THE MISSING PILL

A Park Pals Mystery
Book 2

Dwain Cassady

ISBN: Paperback: 978-1-965576-02-1
eBook: 978-1-965576-03-8
Hardback: 978-1-965576-07-6

THE
MISSING
PILL

CHAPTER 1

She sat, worry weighing her down. She stood, anxiety propelling her into motion. *What am I going to do?*

She was behind on what her boss expected, demanded. The penalty for not delivering was too harsh to pay. *I just can't fail.*

She was pacing now. Walking back and forth in her ratty little trailer, her mind racing to find a way out of her predicament.

She was an undocumented immigrant. When she was twenty-two, her parents and brother had been killed by a drug cartel in Palenque, Mexico. She never found out why. Maybe the cartel thought they had seen a drug deal. Maybe they just decided to kill people that day. She would never know because they would never be prosecuted.

Fearing for her life, she had fled, using all of her savings to get to Gainesville, Georgia. Her uncle, Pablo, lived there. By the time she arrived, he was in jail, awaiting his deportation hearing. He had been apprehended during a traffic stop.

María found herself all alone in a strange country with no money. She didn't like the terms of employment, but this job was the only one she had found. Actually, the job had found her. She had been sleeping on a bench when a woman shook her awake and offered her the job.

She wiped the tears flowing down her face and stomped her foot, terrifying the cat that had just rubbed against her leg.

I have to do what I have to do.

CHAPTER 2

*O*nly *good things can happen on a day like this,* Fitz Fitzgerald thought as he pulled into Laurel Park. Dawn painted the eastern sky a glorious pink, promising a great day.

Zee Jameson pulled into the park a few minutes behind Fitz. The two residentially challenged men lived out of their cars and came to the bathhouse in the park each morning to do their necessary ablutions.

"Mornin', Zee!" Fitz said, coming out of the bathroom with a fresh bowl of water for his ginger cat, Buffett.

Zee moaned and groaned as he worked his tall, skinny frame out of the car. "These old joints are stiff and sore. They get worse every day."

"At least it's a beautiful morning."

"That it is. Cain't complain about the weather."

"Or the view." Fitz's eyes drifted around the park where the Bradford pears were putting on a show in the spring dawn's light.

"You stay put, King," Zee directed his small dog. "I'll be right back. No barking." He made his way into the bathhouse.

Fitz stretched, ran his fingers through his long salt-and-pepper beard, then noticed headlights bouncing over a speed hump. Ben Blessing parked his Outback two spaces down from Fitz's old Highlander. Ben was in his early seventies and had white hair and a neatly trimmed beard.

"Good morning," Ben called, getting out of his car. "It's a marvelous day."

"Hey, Ben," Fitz returned.

"Katía and Luna aren't here yet?"

"Haven't seen them, but it's still early."

Ben walked to the passenger side and leashed up Snickers, his brown labradoodle. "Come on, Snickers. It's workout time."

Snickers hopped out and pulled to get to Fitz, sniffing hands and pockets. Fitz offered pets and said, "Zee'll be out in a minute. I'm sure he has treats."

Snickers whined at the sound of her favorite word. When Zee came out, she barked and dragged Ben over.

"Here ya go, girl. You know who loves you." He handed over a dog bone.

"Are we waiting on Katía and Luna or hitting the trail?" Ben asked.

"My joints ain't gonna make it today," Zee said.

"Walking's the best thing for them, Zee. Come on," Ben coaxed.

"King needs the exercise, too," Fitz added.

"OK, but we're gonna have to move slow," Zee said.

"There's a new Corvette in the upper parking lot. I wonder whom it belongs to," Ben said.

"It must have come in after I got here," Fitz replied. "We'll have to check it out when we walk by. … I wonder who that could be," Fitz grinned, jutting his chin toward two more sets of headlights coming toward them.

Luna pulled in with Katía right behind. "¡Buenos días, guys!" Luna Castillo called, getting out of her 4Runner. She was a sixty-year-old Latina who was a retired teacher.

Fitz braced himself as Katía Bancroft exited her Prius. Her black hair was tamed with a baseball cap that said, "4given." She had taken to hugging everyone since the ordeal last winter where she had allowed herself to be abducted by the Confederate Rising gang and things had gone wrong. Being in the clutches of the gang that was kidnapping Black people for Dr. Max Herringer's illegal experiments had given her a deeper appreciation of everyday life. She no longer took anything for granted.

Fitz was getting more comfortable with the hugs, but it still took some mental preparation.

"Good morning, park pals! This is the day that the Lord has made, and I'm going to rejoice and be glad in it," Katía said as she made the rounds hugging everyone.

Fitz didn't hesitate to return the hug. *This is getting easier.*

Another change Katía had made since her abduction was to walk with the group till she got to the spot from which she wanted to photograph that day. With dawn blooming in the eastern sky, the five-some plus two dogs and a cat set off toward the trail that encircled the park along the lake.

"You look like you're struggling today, Zee," Luna observed.

"Yeah, old Arthur's misbehavin' this mornin'. Y'all might want to go on and leave me behind."

"Nope. We're sticking with you," Ben said.

Fitz tugged at his beard. *This is going to be a slow walk.*

"You need to trim that beard, make it look nice like mine," Zee quipped, stroking his neatly trimmed beard. The group laughed.

"You're just jealous," Fitz responded, but the comment did get him to thinking. *Maybe I do need to tidy myself up a bit.*

Matching their paces to Zee's, the group moved down the path. "Incoming runner," Ben called.

Fitz looked up to see a woman barreling down on them. He and Luna stepped to the right to make room for her to pass.

The woman, sixtyish, blond hair, and chiseled cheek bones grunted, "Hey," as she passed.

"Good mornings," chased her down the trail.

Rounding the curve nearest to the lake, they were greeted with a blaze of pink and orange shining in the east.

"That's my cue," Katía said and took off at a trot toward a point out by the water. She already had the camera set up on its tripod when the group caught up.

"I don't think a picture can do this justice," Ben said, marveling at the sunrise.

"True, but I'm going to give it my best shot," Katía replied, hurrying to adjust settings on the camera.

As they proceeded, Fitz wrestled with a conflict in his heart. *Luna wants to walk fast, but Zee has to move slow. How can I make them both happy?* The thought nagged at him as they continued along the trail even though Luna seemed perfectly content.

Topping the rise that brought them along the upper parking lot, Fitz forgot to walk when his eyes caught the white Corvette.

"Like a deer in the headlights," Ben teased when he noticed Fitz had stopped. Zee was right beside Fitz.

"Are you ogling the woman or the car?" Luna quipped.

Fitz hadn't noticed the woman. "The car, Luna."

The woman, the jogger who had passed them earlier, was bent double, chin near her knees, stretching her hamstrings.

"Ouch. That hurts just lookin' at her," Zee said.

Ben crossed the narrow strip of grass between the asphalt trail and the parking lot. "Good morning. Your car is amazing."

The woman unfolded her body into standing and regarded him with intense blue eyes and no hint of a smile. After a pause, she seemed to decide he was harmless and said, "Thank you. She's my baby."

Ben approached a few more steps. "We're regulars at the park, and this is the first time I've seen you. I hope you enjoy visiting."

"I did. It was a nice run."

Ben took a couple steps more, and without a word the woman hurried into her car and cranked it up. Ben hustled back onto the grass when he realized she was backing up.

"She's quite the looker, Fitz," Luna teased.

"A bit lacking in personality, though," Ben added.

CHAPTER 3

Fitz stood, rooted to that spot on the trail until the Corvette was out of sight. "One of these days I'd love to drive one of those, even if it's just for one trip around town."

"Hey, we should save our money, put it together, and rent one!" Zee said, rubbing his hands together.

"I doubt they'd rent one to a residentially challenged person," Fitz moaned.

"They'd rent one to me," Ben grinned.

"You guys are too much. A beautiful, apparently single woman was here, and you're drooling over the car," Luna chuckled

"I should have asked her out. She might let me drive," Zee stated.

Fitz didn't say anything. He had withdrawn into himself. *Luna's right. She was good looking. No! I can't have thoughts like these. I'm betraying Sharon.* He shook his head. "We need to get moving."

The trail led them around the tennis courts and down a steep incline. Luna held Zee's arm as they descended. At the bottom of the hill, Fitz heard weeping. Apparently the others heard it too since everyone looked at each other and the conversation stopped.

"That can't be good," Ben said.

The weeping turned to wailing.

"Someone's in trouble. Let's go," Luna said and picked up the pace.

The others hurried along with her, except for Zee. Fitz lagged behind, waiting for him.

"Go see what's goin' on. I'll be there soon," Zee directed.

The wailing was emanating from a woman sitting in a hammock swing facing the lake. Luna, Fitz, and Ben stopped on the trail. Snickers tugged at her leash, pulling toward the crying woman. Ben held her back. Buffett sat down and licked his paw.

"Snickers is right. We should check on her," Luna whispered. She walked over and stood a few feet away. "Hola," she said to the woman, who was Latina. The woman buried her head in her hands and continued to wail.

Zee caught up with the group. "She sounds bad."

Luna stepped closer. "Hey, what's wrong? I'll help if I can."

The woman jumped as if she hadn't realized Luna was there. She eyed Luna through puffy eyes, her body jerking with hitched breaths as she cried. The woman was short, maybe hitting five feet, and her feet didn't touch the ground from the swing.

She slid forward so her feet would touch in order to turn to face Luna. The hitches in her breath slowed. She finally took a deep breath and croaked out, "I'm going to die." She burst into weeping again, and her face landed in her hands.

Luna looked to the park pals, then back at the woman. Fitz dug his hands into his pockets. *I'm glad Luna's the one talking to her.*

Luna crept forward and placed her hand on the woman's shoulder. "Tell me what's wrong."

The woman took several deep breaths, and her sobbing slowed. Finally she was able to say, "She stole my purse. It had my medicine in it. I die without it." The tears continued to flow, and she looked at Luna with pleading eyes.

"Maybe we can help you get more medicine," Luna offered.

"No. I no can get more medicine. I will die."

"Why not? My friends and I will be happy to help. Tell me the whole story." Luna pulled tissues from the little waist pack in which she carried her phone and handed them over.

The woman fought to bring her sobbing under control. She wiped her face three times with the tissues. As she glanced at the other park pals, a worried expression crossed her face.

"It's fine. They're friends of mine," Luna said.

"I'm afraid to tell," the woman said.

"I can't help you if I don't know what's going on," Luna coaxed.

"I had the kidney transplant in Mexico City four months ago. Mi esposo y hija, I mean husband and daughter, came here two years ago to make a better life. When my daughter had appendicitis and surgery, I came to care for her so mi esposo no lose his job. I had the Prograf pills in my purse when a woman stole it. Without them I will die."

"What do those pills do?" Luna asked.

"They are immunosuppressants. They keep me from rejecting the new kidney."

Fitz cringed at the woman's story. Even Buffett seemed to take note, pulling Fitz over and rubbing on her leg.

"That's terrible," Luna said. "How long ago was your purse stolen?"

"Yesterday afternoon. I missed two pills."

"What did the police say? Is there any way they can help with the medicine?"

"I no can call police." The woman searched Luna's face with pleading eyes. "Is there any way you can help?"

Luna looked to the park pals.

"There has to be something we can do," Ben said. "Can your doctor send a prescription here?"

"No, the law won't allow a doctor from Mexico to prescribe drugs here," Fitz pointed out. "Ask her where the purse was stolen. A lot of times thieves will grab the wallet and toss the purse out the window. Maybe we can find it."

The woman scrunched up her eyes and looked to Luna. "Why he talk to you? It was stolen in the parking lot of One Twenty-nine Salvage. She took it and ran. I did not see a car."

"Which way did she run?" Luna asked.

"Down the road next to the store."

"What's your name? Mine's Luna."

"Me llamo Victoria."

"It's nice to meet you, Victoria. Would you like us to help you look for that purse?"

"OK. I was too shocked to chase her. Besides, she was young. I no could catch her."

"Come on. Let's go see if we can find those pills," Luna said, holding her hand out.

Victoria took her hand and stood.

"Where's your car?" Ben asked.

"I no have a car. I walked."

"You can ride with me, then," Luna said. "We're parked right over there."

The hammock swings were located near the bathhouse from which the park pals had started their walk. They led Victoria across the grass to the parking lot.

"Do the rest of you want to ride with me?" Ben offered.

"I'd love to," Zee said. "I always enjoy a fancy ride."

"Three people, two dogs, and a cat might be a bit much," Fitz noted. "Besides, I need to let Katía know that we're leaving. Y'all go ahead."

"Good thinking," Ben said. "I wouldn't want to leave her behind. Maybe the two of you should ride together."

Fitz headed toward where Katía had set up her camera, popping three dark chocolate M&Ms into his mouth on the way. *It's going to be harder to keep these when the weather gets hot.*

He called to Katía from the trail and explained Victoria's situation. "We're going to One Twenty-nine Salvage to walk the roads to see if we can find it."

"Mission Missing Pill. I'm in. Just let me get my camera put up."

Fitz and Buffett waited while she removed her camera from the tripod and stowed it in the bag.

"I got some great shots this morning. I'll have to show them to you when we get a chance," Katía said.

"I'd love to see them," Fitz replied. "I hope we can find those pills. She's afraid she'll die without them."

"From what I've heard, every dose of immunosuppressant a transplant patient misses increases their chance of rejecting the organ. We have to find that purse."

They walked back across the grass, taking a straight line to their cars. Buffett trotted along just ahead.

"Buffett seems like a smart cat. It's always like he knows exactly where we're going," Katía noted.

"I'm sure he's smarter than I am."

Katía laughed. "You might be right."

"Hey, I resemble that remark."

"Come on. I'll bring you back after we find that purse."

Fitz popped three more M&Ms into his mouth and followed Buffett into Katía's Prius.

"My driving doesn't stress you out that bad, does it?" Katía quipped.

Fitz stammered, "I… It… No."

The others were milling around the empty parking lot when Fitz and Katía arrived.

"It's a good thing the store isn't open yet. The parking lot's usually full," Fitz said. "You'd better stay in the car," he directed to Buffett. "And behave. This isn't our car."

"Meow."

"Shall we split up and cover more ground?" Ben asked.

"That's a good idea," Luna said. "Do you feel like walking, Victoria?"

"Sí."

"OK, Victoria and I will take Pass Circle."

"Let's go north on Cleveland Highway," Katía said, giving Fitz's arm a tug.

"I don't think this old knee is gonna tolerate that walk," Zee said.

"That's fine. You mind the dogs, and I'll take south on Cleveland Highway," Ben said.

"What did the purse look like?" Katía asked.

"I have a picture. My daughter made it for me. I mean she decorated it with the beads," Victoria said, pulling up a photo on her phone and passing it around. "I'm glad I had my phone in my pocket when she stole my purse."

"Oh, that's beautiful," Luna said when she saw the photo.

The purse was brown leather with tassels, some of which had been strung with beads in the form of a V. The group split up and began their search.

"I'm not sure we're going to be able to get across the road," Katía said, eyeing the endless stream of vehicles heading toward Gainesville.

"Sure we will," Fitz said. He eyed a small break in the cars, walked to the middle of the road and held up his hand. The car slowed, allowing them to cross.

"I get the feeling you've done that before," Katía said.

"A time or two."

They walked along the side of the road scanning the ditch and bank. When Lakeland Road was across from them, Fitz said, "I think they would have tossed it by now. Let's head back."

Victoria burst into tears when everyone returned empty-handed.

CHAPTER 4

While he waited for Victoria to regain her composure, Fitz peeked into Katía's Prius to check on Buffett and to give himself time to think. *There has to be something we can do. She needs that medicine.*

He walked back to the group and heard Luna saying, "I think you need to go to the emergency room. That's probably your best chance for getting the medicine."

"No. No. I no can go there. I have no documents. I have no money."

"They'll treat you whether or not you can pay," Ben said.

"They will arrest me. I no can do that."

"Unfortunately, being in jail might be your best option for getting the medicine you need," Fitz stated.

"Fitz!" Katía scolded.

Victoria sobbed again.

"What about Good News Clinic?" Zee suggested.

"That's a great idea, Zee," Katía said. "I bet they would help without asking about documentation. What do you think, Fitz?"

"I believe you're right about not checking for documentation. It's not your everyday medicine though, so they might not have it on hand," Fitz replied.

"That sounds like our best next step," Ben said, checking his watch. "I have to get going. I have a doctor's appointment at nine."

"Katía, can you take her? I have a dentist appointment at ten," Luna said.

Katía opened her phone and paused. She looked to Fitz with pleading eyes. "I have a district meeting this morning."

"Can your husband take you?" Fitz asked.

"No. He no can leave work."

Fitz looked to the ground, then the sky. "OK. You need to get there soon. I'll take you if you think you can stand riding in my car." He popped three M&Ms into his mouth.

"Thanks, Fitz. You've got this," Katía said, patting him on the shoulder.

I can't ask Zee to go with us. There's no room in the car. What have I done?

"Come on. I'll take y'all back to the park," Katía said, indicating Zee, Fitz, and Victoria. Ben and Luna got into their cars and left.

During the short ride back to the park, Victoria pulled her phone from her pocket. "I tell my husband I go to get medicine with you," she said while entering a text.

Her phone pinged and she smiled. "He worries you will rape me. I told him you are old."

"Gee, thanks," Fitz said with a laugh.

Back at the park, Fitz let Buffett jump into the back seat then cleared the passenger seat for Victoria. "Are you afraid of cats?" he asked.

"I love cats," she replied, before sitting down.

Fitz popped three more M&Ms into his mouth while walking around the car. By the time he sat down, Buffett was purring in Victoria's lap as she stroked his fur. Fitz started to scold Buffett but noticed Victoria looked calmer.

After about five minutes of silence, Victoria asked, "What is this clinic?"

"Good News Clinic is a free service to the community for people who can't afford healthcare," Fitz explained. "The people there are great. I've used it before."

"They no ask for documentation?"

"I'm sure not. They didn't ask for mine."

"You no look foreign, though." She was petting Buffett rapidly.

"If you're that worried, I'll go in and ask first," Fitz said, hoping to calm her back down.

"And they no charge money?"

"No, it's free."

Fitz noticed Buffett relax as the petting slowed in intensity.

After verifying that the clinic wouldn't ask about her immigration status, Fitz led Victoria inside. The intake worker listened to her story with a concerned look. She entered her demographic information, then said, "That's going to be an issue for our pharmacist." She sent them to the other side of the building to talk with him.

Victoria pulled three tissues from the box on the counter as they exited. Fitz pulled out three more M&Ms.

"The next question is, will they have the medicine on hand?" Fitz said.

The tears flowed faster. *I wish I hadn't said that.*

A tall, thin man walked toward them. "Hi, I'm Allen Carmichael. I'm the pharmacist here. How can I help you?"

Victoria related her story again. Fitz noticed the concern forming on Allen's brow.

After Victoria finished, Allen said, "I'm afraid we don't have any of that type of medication on hand. The best we can do is apply to the pharmaceutical company's program for uninsured patients."

Fitz's hope grew until Allen's next statement.

"Unfortunately, it will take two to four weeks to get approved for the program and actually get the medicine."

Victoria plopped into a chair and covered her face with the tissues, her shoulders jerking up and down.

"Do you have any other ideas?"

"She really needs that medicine now. She could see if her doctor in Mexico could write a new prescription and get a family member to mail it overnight. It would be costly, because insurance probably won't cover it. I'm sorry, Victoria. I wish I could help more."

Victoria nodded her head.

"Let's go ahead and fill out the form for the pharmaceutical company. That can be in the works while we come up with a more immediate plan." Fitz suggested.

"Good idea," Allen said. He directed them to a computer where she could fill out the needed form.

Fitz's mind churned while Victoria worked on the computer. *This isn't good enough. Her body could start rejecting the kidney before she gets the medicine. What else can I do?* His angst called for more M&Ms.

Victoria settled into the car, and Fitz realized she was going to need more tissues. "I'll run in and grab some more tissues."

When he was walking out the door, tissues in hand, an idea struck. *Why didn't I think of that before?*

CHAPTER 5

Fitz handed Victoria the handful of tissues then said, "Come on, we're going to see the doctor."

He led her back into the clinic and explained to the intake lady that they needed to see the doctor.

"OK. Have a seat and we'll call her back when it's time."

Fitz sat down one seat over from Victoria and explained his plan. "Tell the doctor your story and see if he or she will give you a prescription. We'll go by the pharmacy and find out how much it would cost to get the pills without insurance. Then we'll try to figure out a way to come up with the money."

Victoria peeked over the tissues. Fitz thought he could see the trace of a smile.

While Victoria was back with the doctor, Fitz pulled up the newspaper on his phone. One story caught his attention: BODY FOUND IN DUMPSTER AT CONSTRUCTION SITE.

Pulling up the article, Fitz read: "The body of a young Latina woman was found in the dumpster at the construction site of a new apartment complex in Oakwood. The woman appears to have been in her mid to late twenties. So far, there are no missing person reports matching her description. If anyone in the community has information regarding her, please contact the police immediately." A sketch artist's rendering of the woman's face showed her alive and lovely.

That's just sick. Why do people have to kill each other? It was probably some crazed druggie who raped her and then killed her. I'd like to be the one who tracks him down.

Victoria walked back with puffy eyes, a smile, and a prescription in hand. Fitz thought about showing her the picture from the article to see if she knew the woman but decided it might start the tears again.

Back in the car, Fitz's phone pinged. He opened the text from Luna. "Any luck?"

"Making progress," he sent back. Sending texts was not his thing. Walgreens was in the direction back toward Victoria's house, so Fitz elected to go there.

"Remember to tell the clerk you just want to find out how much twenty-eight pills will cost. That should cover you till the program kicks in," Fitz coached.

Viviana nodded her head and opened the car door. When Fitz didn't open his door, she asked, "You no coming?"

"OK," he said. He was planning to sit in the car and wait but sensed she needed him for backup.

When the pharmacy assistant called them forward, Victoria froze. Fitz waited for her to move. When he realized that wasn't happening, he took the prescription out of her hand and approached the counter.

"This lady has a prescription she needs to get filled. Someone stole her purse with her supply of pills, so it's urgent that she get the medicine. She doesn't have insurance, so she wants to find out what the cost would be," he explained.

The assistant disappeared back to where the pharmacist worked. In a couple of minutes, she returned and said, "The generic will be ninety-two forty-six for a thirty-day supply."

Fitz's mouth dropped open. It was his turn to freeze. He couldn't believe they were actually affordable.

The pharmacy assistant tilted her head and raised her eyebrows. "So would you like us to fill it?"

"Definitely. We'll wait." He looked back to find Victoria rummaging through her purse.

She looked up with terror in her eyes. "I only have five dollars."

"No problem," Fitz said. "I'm happy to pay for them."

Fitz had trouble reading her expression, then realized she was about to cry again.

"I no can believe you do that. You are so kind."

"Knowing you'll be OK will be a lot easier on me than worrying about the alternative," Fitz answered.

While they sat and waited for the prescription to be filled, Fitz stared at his phone. *I can do this.* He pulled three M&Ms from his pocket and opened the text app. There were two threads. One was the group that Ben had created last winter during their battle with Dr. Max Herringer's thugs. The other was the individual message from Luna that had come that morning.

Fortified with the M&Ms, he opened the group text. "We are getting a prescription filled for the medicine. She should be OK."

"What are you doing?" Victoria asked.

"I'm letting the other folks who were helping this morning know that you're getting the medicine."

"You are kind people. In Mexico, they say all Americans are greedy. I see that is not true."

"We do have our share of that type, though," Fitz answered.

After Fitz paid with his debit card, he hunted down the water fountain so Victoria could take a pill before they left.

"You need to go ahead and get that into your system," he explained.

While she swallowed the pill, Fitz's phone started pinging with responses to the text he had sent. He looked at the emojis and GIFs. *How did they do that?*

"I have to tell my husband," Victoria said, pulling out her phone. On the way to the car her phone pinged. "He says to tell you thank you, and he will pay you back as soon as he can."

Fitz was tongue tied with conflicting thoughts. *I don't want them to pay me back. I could use the money. It might be a source of pride, and he needs to pay me back. What do I say?* "It doesn't matter if you pay me back. I was happy to help."

He dropped Victoria off at her house, then headed for his usual Wednesday visit to the library.

CHAPTER 6

That afternoon, Katía readied herself to visit one of her parishioners. Helen Brown was a piece of work. One of the wealthiest members of her congregation, she was quite kind and generous but keen for attention and prone to gossip. It took some willpower to make it through a visit with her.

Katía parked in front of the two-story brick home with its three-car garage and thought, *I could get used to that.* There was a van parked at the curb with a magnetic sign that read, "Sparkles." *That's a cute name. Must be a cleaning service.*

She psyched herself up for the visit, knowing Helen would go on and on about the knee replacement surgery she had had three weeks ago. Katía knew that because she had already been to see Helen twice since the surgery.

She rang the doorbell and waited, hearing the walker clatter across the hardwood floor. *I meant to bring her some tennis balls to put on the bottom of her walker.* Katía scolded herself till the door opened.

"Hey, pastor! It's so nice to see you. Come on in," Helen said.

"How are you feeling today, Helen?"

"Now, honey, let me tell you. I've been hurtin' so bad. This surgery has been hard on this old woman. My old knee will go to throbbin', and it's all I can do to keep from hollerin' out. It was just about all I could do to get to the door." Katía noticed that she easily closed the door and led her back to the den with no limp.

"Have a seat and let's talk. It's good to have someone come to see me. I hardly ever get to talk to anyone these days, being confined like I am, you know. Can I get you some tea?"

Katía could hear the vacuum running upstairs. "It sounds like your cleaning lady is here."

"She sure is. I couldn't make it without her. My old joints would never survive cleanin' this big ole place, honey. And she's just the nicest thing, always smilin' and takin' time to talk. If you decide you want a house cleaner, I highly recommend her." She rubbed her knee and grimaced, letting out a soft moan.

"I'll keep that in mind," Katía said, knowing there was no way she could afford a housekeeper. *She knows that too, since she knows how much the church pays me.*

Helen straightened in her chair and leaned forward just a bit. "Now tell me the news. What's going on in the church that I've missed?"

"Joyce's cancer is back. She's going to the doctor next Wednesday to find out what they're going to do."

"Honey, I've already heard that and been prayin' for her. How about some juicy news? Anybody cheatin' on their wife? That kind of thing." She eyed Katía expectantly.

Katía tried to find something that would satisfy Helen and decided to tell her about the woman whose pills had been stolen. "We ran across a woman at the park this morning. She was crying. It turns out, a woman had stolen her purse in the One Twenty-nine Salvage store parking lot. We tried to find her purse but couldn't."

"Hang on just a minute, honey. My knee is killin' me. I need a pain pill. I'll be right back." With moans and groans, Helen pried herself from her chair and headed toward the kitchen.

Katía couldn't help shaking her head as Helen walked away. *As soon as the conversation turned away from her, she needed a pain pill.* She got up and surveyed the books in the book case, noting several novels that she had read.

Katía heard muttering coming from the kitchen. "I only have twelve left. I'll run out before I see the surgeon again. I must have taken more than I thought. What am I going to do?"

Helen looked dejected when she walked back into the den.

"Everything OK?" Katía asked.

"I'm afraid I'll run out of pain pills before I can get a refill. This thing hurts so bad, I don't know what I'm going to do."

"Did you take more than you were supposed to?" *I want to tell her that's a bad thing to do, but I don't think she needs a lecture right now.*

Helen eased back into her chair. "I don't remember cheatin' like that. I usually write down the time and date when I take a pain pill. The old memory must be slippin' because I don't see a record of takin' any extra pills."

Katía felt for Helen. "I'm sorry to hear that. Maybe your knee will get less painful before you run out."

"Oh, honey, that would be nice. But the way this thing hurts, I don't expect it to ever get better. What am I goin' to do?"

Helen seemed genuinely worried this time. Katía decided praying would be the best thing. "I think it's time we prayed, Helen."

"That would be nice, pastor. Thank you."

"Let's pray. Dear loving God, thank you so much for your Holy Spirit that walks with us like a shepherd through all we go through. We pray you will be especially close to Helen. Help her knee to heal and become less painful and give her the strength she needs to overcome this challenge in her life. Amen."

"Amen," Helen echoed.

When Katía looked up, a young Latina woman was standing quietly at the door of the den.

"That was a nice prayer. I'm all done. Is there anything else you need before I go?" she said with a smile.

"You're such an angel, María. Thank you so much. I have your money here."

Katía watched as the woman walked across the room and received an envelope. When María put the envelope into her purse, Katía stiffened. It looked like the one in Victoria's photo. *Should I say anything? I can't accuse her of stealing the purse. It could just be a common purse that a lot of folks from Mexico have.*

When María was nearly out of the den, Katía said, "I love your purse. It's beautiful."

"Thank you," María answered, then turned and left.

Katía couldn't help herself. As soon as María closed the front door, she said, "Her purse looks just like the one that was stolen from that lady at the park."

"María is too nice to be stealin' purses," Helen said. "I don't believe she would ever do that."

"I wonder if she could have found it after the thief discarded it."

"I suppose that's possible. I can't say I've ever paid any attention to her purse, so I can't say how long she's had it. But anyway, please get the church prayin' for me. I'm goin' to need all the prayers I can get to get through this."

"Trust me, they're already praying. We lifted you up Sunday."

"Thanks. Just make sure they all know how much I'm hurtin'. This is goin' to be a battle."

"I certainly will let them know. Is there anything I can do before I leave?"

"Would you mind grabbin' me a water out of the fridge? It would save me some painful steps."

"I'll be happy to." Katía delivered the bottle of water.

"Would it be terrible to ask you to pour it into a glass with lots of ice? I like it so much better that way."

"No, I'll be glad to." *I wonder why she didn't tell me that to start with. I guess anything to drag the visit out a little longer.*

After delivering the water, including a paper towel as a coaster, Katía made her exit. She blew out a deep breath as she made her way to the car, relieved that she had done her good deed for the day.

CHAPTER 7

The next morning, Fitz went through his morning routine at the park. The sun was considering getting out of bed and had just begun to pull back the covers of darkness. He had bathed, replenished Buffett's water, and scooped the litter when he heard Ben's car rolling in.

"I'm thankful for another day to spend with our friends, aren't you?" he said to his ginger cat.

"Meow."

"Let's get your harness on so we can walk with the crew."

"Meow." Buffett stood still while Fitz buckled the harness.

Fitz rubbed down his back. "Buffett, I don't know what I'd do without you. You're such a good cat, and you always seem to know how to take care of me."

"It's mighty early for a smile like that," Ben said, straightening up as he got out of the car.

"I guess I'm feeling good after being able to help that woman yesterday."

Snickers bounded out of the car and ran to greet Fitz and Buffett. Buffett jumped to the ground and rubbed around Snickers' legs while she sniffed.

"Hey, girl," Fitz said, giving Snickers a back scratch.

"Taking Victoria around until you got the medicine was really kind of you. I think that's the first time I've known of your letting another human get into your car."

"There's a first time for everything. … Actually, Luna hopped in last winter while we were hunting for Katía and Zee."

"Wow! Are you sure you're Fitz? Do I know you?"

Fitz laughed. "Maybe I'm mellowing out in my old age."

More car lights bounced over the speed bump, signaling Katía's and Luna's arrivals.

"Good morning!" Luna chirped. "How's our local hero?"

Fitz's cheeks warmed. *I'm glad it's dark.*

"I agree," Katía said. "You saved Victoria's life, Fitz. I think we should call the paper and get them to run a story on what you did." Katía grabbed Fitz in a hug.

"All we need is Zee, and we can get on with our walk," Fitz responded, trying to deflect the attention off him.

"That's a great idea, Katía," Luna said. "I bet the paper would love to do a story on what Fitz did yesterday."

"Yeah! We could call that reporter who helped us out last winter," Ben added. "What was her name?"

"Serena," Fitz answered. "But I'm not doing an interview about this."

"What do you mean, a reporter helped you out?" Katía asked.

"We got the Times to put out the story about your abduction on line to help spread the word so we could find you," Ben replied.

"Wow. Somehow I missed that. Y'all really did do a lot to rescue me."

"We tried everything we could think of," Ben said.

The group went quiet. Fitz retreated into his memory of the awful events last February. Losing Katía to the abductors after she posed as a residentially challenged person in their effort to find Zee had been terrifying. They ended up discovering that a doctor was performing illegal medical experiments on Black people.

"It's about time," Fitz said, noticing Zee's headlights coming toward them.

Zee groaned getting out of his car. "This chilly weather wreaks havoc on my joints. Good mornin'. everyone." He stood up, stretched, then zipped his jacket against the chilly forty-seven-degree breeze. "I hope y'all haven't been waiting long."

"Nope. We've just been trying to convince Fitz to get an article published in the paper about how he helped Victoria yesterday," Katía replied.

"Not a good idea," Zee said with a grin. "That mug on the first page would be bad PR for the county."

With a laugh the five people, two dogs, and a cat set off along the trail.

"You should bring Snow and Cotton to join the menagerie," Ben said.

"I don't think they'd like it. They're indoor cats," Katía answered, referring to her two white kitties.

"Yeah, they might get ideas about what else is out there in this big ole world," Zee added.

The group came around where the trail crossed the road. The sun had risen just enough for them to make out a woman walking down the road. She was waving.

"Who's that?" Ben wondered.

"I think it's Victoria," Katía answered.

"Is she holding a basket? Maybe there's food in there," Zee said, rubbing his hands together.

The woman waved again.

"Should we wait for her?" Ben asked.

"I know I'm waiting," Zee replied. He led the way back off the road and onto the trail. "I can't wait to see what's in that basket."

"You're as bad as Yogi Bear," Ben laughed.

They waited as the woman drew closer, and they could make out for sure that she was Victoria.

"Good morning," Katía called.

"¡Buenos días!" Victoria called, quickening her pace. "I want to thank you for saving my life. I make conchas." She pulled back the towel in the basket to reveal delicious looking pastries topped with cinnamon and sugar.

"Yum! That smells heavenly," Zee said.

"Thank you, Victoria. That is very kind of you," Luna added.

"There's a picnic table a little ways down. Shall we set up shop there?" Ben suggested.

As they gathered around the picnic table, Victoria also pulled out a thermos of coffee, cups, plates, napkins, creamer, and sugar along with the conchas.

"That's just like Mary Poppins' bag," Ben noted.

"I no can thank you enough," Victoria said, placing a hand on Fitz's shoulder. "My husband says he pay you back when he can."

"Don't worry about that. I was happy to help," Fitz answered. He took a bite. "Wow! That's wonderful!"

"I didn't think about the cost of the pills," Luna said. "Let us help you out with that. How much were they?"

Ben and Katía nodded, absorbed in chewing their first bites of the conchas.

"It's OK. I took care of it," Fitz said, taking a sip of coffee.

"It was ninety-two dollars. My husband pay him back," Victoria stated.

Ben pulled out his wallet. If we divide that up four ways, it's about… twenty-three dollars apiece. That's not bad for saving a life!" He offered Fitz twenty-five dollars.

"My purse is in the car," Luna said, "But I'll give you money when we get back."

"Me, too," Katía said.

Fitz was stuck. He took another bite of the concha to buy some time. When he swallowed he said, "You don't have to do that." *I could eat better this month if I take it.*

"Nonsense. Twenty dollars won't hurt any of us, but ninety-two puts a big hole in your finances," Ben said, pushing the money closer to Fitz.

Fitz swallowed his pride along with another bite of concha. "OK, if you put it that way." He took the cash.

"Now you and your husband don't have to worry about the money," Luna said.

"You people are too kind," Victoria said, tears filling her eyes and slowly spilling over.

"Oh!" Katía held up a finger as she took a sip of coffee. "I saw a lady with a purse that looked a lot like yours yesterday."

"I don't think it was mine. There is only one like mine. My daughter made it for me. The beads form my initial."

"Are you sure, because this looked a lot like the picture," Katía answered.

"I show you," Victoria said, wiping her cheeks and opening her phone to the photo of the purse. "Other purses like this have tassels. No beads."

Katía took the phone and studied it. "The purse I saw looked just like that, beads and all."

Silence washed over the group, each person stopping at different points in consuming the conchas and coffee.

After a moment, Fitz said, "Let's not go jumping to conclusions. Can you describe the woman who snatched your purse?"

"She was a young Latina. Flaca… Skinny. It happened fast. I saw her back while she ran away."

"The woman I saw was a young Latina. She is the cleaning lady for one of my parishioners," Katía said.

"Still, unless someone else decorated a purse like that, this could be Victoria's," Luna stated.

"Do you know if the woman's name started with a V? Fitz asked.

"Her name was María," Katía answered.

"Sounds like we've found our thief," Zee said.

"Not necessarily. If it is Victoria's purse, this woman could have found it where the thief threw it out," Fitz observed.

"I noticed she is with Sparkles Cleaning Service," Katía added.

Zee finished his concha and peered into the basket. There were three left. He looked at Victoria with pleading eyes.

"Have another," she said, sliding the basket closer to him.

He scanned the rest of the group.

"Go ahead. It's OK," Luna coaxed. "We need to get Victoria's purse back. Any ideas?"

CHAPTER 8

Crystal Samson signed her five-hundred-dollar check with a flourish, placed it in the envelope, and sealed it up. This check reserved her spot at the annual charity gala at the Chattahoochee Country Club. *It's a lot of money, but I really have to put in an appearance. Everyone who's anybody will be there.*

While she grumbled about the cost, she wouldn't miss the event. Rubbing elbows with the county's richest residents was one of her primary joys in life. Even though her business growth had slowed this year, she still had plenty of cash to spend on the event's auction. She paused for a minute, memories of last year's gala floating through her mind.

I just had to outbid Hank in the silent auction for that original statue. He always acts so uppity. I couldn't let him have it.

Crystal didn't actually like the statue. In fact, it was stowed in a closet at home. She did like winning, though, and that was what had propelled her bid so high. She laid the envelope in the outgoing mail bin and headed downstairs for the weekly staff meeting.

Crystal was the owner and manager of Sparkles Cleaning Service, which was headquartered in a two-story brick building on Hilton Drive. She had made it into a successful business, which helped feed her large ego. She provided a cadre of well-trained maids to take care of the wealthiest people in Hall County. She was paid well for their services and expected a lot from her employees. Since the employees were Latina women, undocumented at that, she provided a fleet of vans that carried them to the various homes. It required an elaborate schedule to move them from house to house. Thankfully, her office manager, Shannon Bledsoe, worked out those details. Shannon had also learned to speak Spanish fluently, for which Crystal was also grateful.

So far, she had not had a single complaint of theft. That was partly attributable to the way she pounded the fear of severe retribution into her employees during their onboarding.

She thoroughly enjoyed the weekly staff meetings. All the maids and office staff would gather to hear what she had to say. What she really thrived on was the nervous tension, fear even, on her staff's faces when she entered the room.

She opened the door quickly without breaking stride, swung her long, curly blond hair, and swayed her hips as she walked across the room. When she reached her spot at the head of the room, she remained standing and paused while eying her staff. Shannon stood in a corner to interpret in Spanish.

"Ladies, you know I appreciate the work you do each week. You are what makes this operation hum.

"We do, however, have three complaints this week. Angelica, Ms. Jackson says you didn't place the bedspread straight. Please pay attention to your work.

"Catarina, Ms. Hamilton reported that you missed a spot when vacuuming. I need you to focus. Work quickly but also carefully.

"María, Helen Brown said you missed a spider web in the corner of her den. That it could have been spun after you left is totally impossible," Crystal paused with a smile and quiet snickers flowed through the room. Crystal relished the fact that they were not comfortable enough to laugh out loud.

"Remember, these are fastidious women for whom we're working. I expect you to do your best at every home every day. I don't need to remind you that you have to stay on time. If you're late, you throw off the whole schedule for the day.

"I'm sure I also don't need to remind you that making your quota is not optional." Crystal bore down on them, her gaze communicating that she was dead serious.

After enjoying the tense silence in the room for a few moments, Crystal made her exit, eyes focused straight ahead, posture erect, hips swaying.

CHAPTER 9

The next Wednesday afternoon, Katía prepared to visit Helen Brown again. She had committed herself to making a visit every week until Helen was over her knee surgery. She was beginning to think recovery might not ever happen.

Katía timed her visit in hopes of running into the cleaning lady again. That was the next step in the park pals' attempt to reunite Victoria and her stolen purse.

When she pulled into Helen's driveway, her spirit deflated. *The Sparkles van isn't here.* She checked her watch and saw that she was fifteen minutes earlier than last week. Katía asked the Lord for fortification then headed to Helen's door.

"Good afternoon, Pastor," Helen said, doorknob in one hand and a cane in the other.

"Hello, Helen. How are you doing? Is the knee any better?"

"I'm still in terrible pain," she said with a smile. "It sure is good to see you. Your prayers always help." Helen shut the door and led the way to the den.

Katía noticed there was no limp with Helen's first few steps, then she started limping on that leg. Singing from upstairs lifted Katía's spirits.

"María has taken to singin' today. She must be in a good mood," Helen pointed out. She plopped down into her chair. "I wasn't sure I was goin' to make it back. The physical therapist insisted that I was ready to ditch the walker and use the cane. I'm not so sure, though. I'm tryin', but I keep the walker on standby just in case." She pointed to where it stood in the corner.

"I've been frettin' all week. I'm goin' to run out of pain medicine tomorrow, and I don't see the doctor until Monday. What am I goin' to do? Listen to me, goin' on about my problems. I haven't even asked how you are doin'."

"I'm doing well, thank you. I'm enjoying the beauty of spring with all the flowers blooming and trees putting on their leaves. It's just glorious."

"Do you have any ideas what I could do about my pain medicine? I think I'll just die if I don't have it."

"Have you called the surgeon?"

"No. I don't want him to think I'm one of those druggies."

"I'm sure he won't think that. Just explain that you're going to run out before you see him. Maybe he'll give you a refill. It can't hurt to ask. Why don't you go ahead and call the office while I'm here?" Katía coaxed.

Helen picked up her cell phone and punched it a couple of times. Putting the phone to her ear, she said, "I really shouldn't do this. I should just tough it out."

After disconnecting the call, Helen said, "All I ever get is the voicemail. It sure would be nice to be able to talk to a person."

"Maybe they'll call in enough pills to get you through to Monday," Katía said.

"Honey, they won't call them in. I'll have to go pick up the prescription, carry it to the drugstore, and wait till they get it filled. I'm not sure it'll be worth the hassle."

Katía struggled for a response. *Maybe a change of subject?* "Do you have any trips planned this year?"

"I'm takin' my son and his family on a cruise in July. I sure hope I can make it. That's partly why I had this surgery. I didn't think I could walk around the ship without it. Now I'm not sure I can make it with it."

Katía counted in her head. "That's three months away. I'm sure you'll be fit as a fiddle by then." She added a warm smile, hoping to sell the idea.

"That is a hopeful thought. I wish I shared your optimism. This thing just hurts so much I don't feel like it's ever goin' to get any better."

"Now, Helen, you've already graduated from the walker to the cane. Just think back to how bad it was right after the surgery, and you'll see how far you've come."

Katía tensed at the sound of footsteps on the stairs. *I have to make sure I don't sound accusatory.*

María stopped in the doorway. "Do you need anything else before I go?"

"No, honey, I'm sure you've done an excellent job, as always. Thank you so much," Helen replied.

"You are welcome."

Katía stood and pretended to notice María's purse for the first time. "I really like your purse. Where did you get it?"

María's eyes darted to Helen, then to an empty chair. "No entiendo. No hablo Inglés, señora."

Katía was shocked. María had just spoken English to Helen. She dug into her memory for the Spanish she had learned in high school. "Tu bolso es bonito."

María hugged the purse to her. "Oh, gracias!"

"¿Dónde lo compras?"

"En México."

"I would love to have one like it. Do you think I could order one?" Katía tried.

"No, señora. I buy it from un vendedor ambulante."

"OK. It was worth a try," Katía said, forcing her smile not to fade.

María turned and walked out the door.

"She seemed upset that you asked about her purse," Helen noted.

"I didn't mean to offend her," Katía said, continuing her ruse. *The beads definitely formed a V.*

"It's time for my afternoon tea. Please join me. I usually have chamomile, but I have other options."

Katía held in the groan. "Sure, I'd love to have some tea."

"I'm so happy. Would you mind fixin' it? Just pick out the flavor you like. The cups are in the cabinet right above the basket with the teas."

The next morning, Katía met the park pals for their daily walk.

"Well?" Luna asked as soon as they had gathered.

"Well, what?" Fitz asked.

"Did you talk to the woman about Victoria's purse?"

"I did. She claims she bought it in Mexico. My Spanish isn't great, but I think she said like at a street vendor or sidewalk shop."

"Do you believe her?" Luna asked.

"Not really. Her eyes were shifty. She might have been lying," Katía answered.

"You got to watch those shifty-eyed folks," Zee added.

As they set off down the trail, Ben asked, "Where's your camera?"

"The sky's all grey. The water's all grey. I don't think today is a good day for photography," Katía answered.

"I really want Victoria to get her purse back. What else can we do?" Luna asked.

"It's just a purse. At least she's going to live," Ben noted.

Hands landing on her hips, Luna said, "You just don't understand. It's hers, and it's a special purse. Her daughter made it for her. She deserves to have it back, and if that woman is a thief, then she doesn't deserve it."

"Maybe next week you could sneak in and steal it back," Zee offered. "It would be nice of you to leave what's in it behind, of course."

"I'm not going to steal a purse," Katía replied. "Besides, we don't know for sure if it's Victoria's."

"Did the beads form a V?" Ben asked.

"Yes, they did," Katía answered.

"You said her name was María." Fitz remembered.

"Why would a María buy a purse with a V on it?" Ben mused.

"Maybe it was cheap?" Zee offered.

"You men just don't understand the relationship between a woman and her purse! I say we confront her with the picture of Victoria's purse. Then she can't claim that it's hers," Luna said.

"I want to be there for that. There could be fireworks!" Zee said, rubbing his hands together.

CHAPTER 10

About halfway around the trail that same dreary morning, a light drizzle started to fall on the park pals. The woman jogger they had seen last week came flying by them, with Fitz and Zee scrambling to get to the side to make room.

"The Vette's back!" Zee said, quickening his steps.

Fitz felt a flash of excitement, too. They came up a rise and saw the Corvette in the parking lot.

"I saw one of those in a showroom when I was looking for my last car. It cost over a hundred thousand dollars," Ben said.

"She must be loaded to be driving it," Katía observed.

"I don't guess I'll ever be ownin' one … unless I win the lottery," Zee grinned and rubbed his hands together.

"I know, … there's always hope," Fitz laughed.

"Ya gotta keep hopin' or there ain't much to live for," Zee explained.

"Amen," Katía added.

When the trail crossed the road, Luna said, "I'm taking a shortcut so I don't get soaked."

The other park pals followed as she abandoned the trail and turned down the road.

"Hey, is that Victoria?" Ben asked, noticing a woman standing under the pavilion near their cars.

"I think I see her basket, too," Zee said,

"You would notice that," Fitz laughed.

"A man's gotta eat," Zee replied.

Victoria waved as they approached the pavilion.

I hope she doesn't think she has to bring something every day. I think once was sufficient. Fitz rubbed the drizzle off his face as he stepped under the cover.

"I bring conchas," Victoria said. "I want to celebrate with my friends one more time."

"Thanks," Zee said, rubbing his hands together.

"Why did you say one more time?" Katía asked.

"I got a job," Victoria answered. "My daughter goes back to school Lunes. I go to work."

"Congratulations," Ben replied.

"Are you sure you're strong enough to go to work?" Katía asked.

"My doctor said I can work after eight weeks if I feel good. It makes nine weeks since the surgery. I think I am OK."

"I'm not sure the stress of working will be good for you," Luna said. "It could increase your chances of rejecting the kidney, especially after you just missed a couple of doses of your medicine."

"Yeah, maybe you should call your doctor first," Fitz added, trying to relax the worry that had drawn his eyebrows together.

"That's a good idea, Fitz," Ben added.

"OK. I call him today. I no start till Monday."

"Where are you going to work?" Katía asked.

"Sparkles. I clean houses."

The park pals fell silent. Fitz puzzled as to whether they should tell her about the purse. *I think it's better she know before she runs into the woman.*

"What is it?" Victoria asked, apparently noticing the consternation on the others' faces.

"There's something you should know before you start work," Fitz said.

"Are you sure?" Katía asked.

"Yeah. Just think how she'd feel if she ran into the woman," Fitz answered, sticking his hands into his pockets. The drizzle turned to a soft rain, creating soothing music on the metal roof of the pavilion.

Katía took a deep breath. "I think a woman who works for Sparkles has your purse. I saw her at one of my parishioner's houses yesterday."

Fitz watched as Victoria's eyes widened and her jaw dropped.

She froze for a few seconds, then finally said, "Oh."

"The purse looks just like the one in the photo you showed us, even with beads in the shape of a V. The woman said she bought it in Mexico," Katía continued.

Victoria was still frozen as though she had stepped out of time.

"Are you OK?" Fitz asked.

"I do not know what to do," she said.

"Maybe we can talk to her again before you start work Monday," Luna offered.

Fitz scrunched his eyebrows again. "She obviously doesn't intend to admit she stole… or found the purse," he said.

"She couldn't admit it in front of her client," Luna noted. "It might be different if we talk to her privately."

"How do you propose to do that?" Fitz asked, his brow knitting tighter.

"What if we met her at the Sparkles office after work today?" Luna suggested.

"You don't know what time 'after work' is," Fitz observed. "Plus, you don't know where she will be at the end of the day. Her last house could be anywhere in the county."

"I think a lot of these companies provide transportation between clients' homes," Ben said.

Fitz cut his eyes to Ben, wishing he had not said that. *Now they'll really want to go to the office. Not a good idea.*

"That is true. She told me a van will take me to the houses. I have to get to the office and home on my own," Victoria said.

"See? It won't be so hard. We may have to wait at the office for a while, but she'll show up," Luna pointed out. "If she knows the woman who is the rightful owner of the purse is coming to work there, she might rethink wanting to hang on to it."

"I don't see that going well," Fitz said. "I think we should just let the purse go."

"Fitz, Fitz, Fitz. You just don't understand. Katía, do you want to come with me this afternoon? I say we camp out at the Sparkles office starting at four. I have a plan," Luna grinned.

CHAPTER 11

Katía pulled into the downtown parking deck at 3:45 that afternoon. She found Luna's car on the second floor and pulled into an open space four cars farther down. She waved at Luna as she approached her 4Runner.

"Hey, Luna," she said, opening the door.

Luna pulled a bag off the passenger seat as she answered, "Good afternoon."

"I see you've been shopping," Katía said, pointing to the Belk bag that Luna had laid on the back seat.

"That's my secret weapon," she replied, cranking the car.

"Oh? Tell me about it."

"We can't expect that woman to give up a purse without a replacement, can we?"

"You didn't?"

"I did."

"That was brilliant, Luna. I wish I had thought of offering her a replacement. Can I see it?"

"Sure."

Katía reached back to get the bag. "It has tassels and everything! I think she'll like it." She relaxed, buoyed by Luna's plan.

"I just hope we find her." Luna drove to the Sparkles office on Hilton Drive.

Katía navigated using her phone, directing Luna out Jesse Jewell Parkway to Atlanta Highway, then right onto Hilton. They found Sparkles, and Luna pulled in and parked.

"What if someone comes out and asks us why we're here?" Katía asked, getting nervous.

"We could say we're here to pick up one of the workers," Luna suggested.

"That's almost true. How about if we say we're here to meet María?"

"That might be too true," Luna laughed. "We don't want to get her into trouble."

"What if they ask which worker?"

"I guess we'd have to say María. That is such a common name, there could be a few Marías working here."

They sat waiting. There was only one other car in the parking lot, a burgundy Camry.

"I wonder if anyone is inside," Katía said.

"It looks like Shannon's here," Luna answered, having read the name on the sign designating the parking place as hers.

A couple of other cars pulled in and parked.

"That's a good sign. I hope they're here to pick up other workers," Luna said.

"What if one of them is here to pick up María?" Katía's nerves increased their intensity.

"We'll just have to hope that's not the case."

Katía sat with the next thought that crossed her mind, wondering whether to voice it. She decided that she would chance it. "Luna, I've noticed you seem very adamant about getting this purse back. I'm wondering why you're so invested in this." She watched for Luna's response. She noticed her fingers tighten on her thigh.

"You noticed, huh? When I was a freshman in college, just having moved into the dorm, this guy attacked me one night while I was walking back from class. I think he was trying to rape me, but I fought him off. In the fight, I dropped my purse. He snatched it and ran off laughing at me."

"I'm so sorry, Luna. That must have been terrible."

"My mom bought the purse for me as a present for starting college. I had my favorite stuffed animal, a small mouse, tucked inside. Losing the purse and little Gigi was worse than losing my money and driver's license. I guess Victoria's purse brought all that back to me."

"Tragedies do have a way of following us throughout life and rearing their heads from time to time. I'm sorry you had to go through that."

"It was so long ago, but things like this can still put me right back there. I'll feel better if we can get Victoria's purse back to her."

A Sparkles van pulled into the parking lot, and Katía sat forward in her seat. Luna was doing something on her phone. Katía watched closely as three women got out of the van and went inside. She noticed each woman was carrying a small black bag.

"None of those is María," Katía said with a mix of relief and disappointment. She wasn't looking forward to the confrontation.

"You seem nervous," Luna observed.

"You noticed, huh? I'm worried that María will make a scene. What if she calls the police and tells them we're harassing her?"

"The police would just tell us to leave her alone. If this doesn't work, I guess that's what we'll do."

"What do you mean you guess?" Katía eyed Luna.

"I'll try to let it go if we don't get the purse back today."

The three women from the van popped back out, one after the other.

"That was quick. They must have been clocking out. I wonder what the little black bags were for. They don't have them now." Katía observed.

"I would assume the clients pay them, and they deliver the money to the office in those bags," Luna replied.

"That makes sense." Katía leaned back and tried to relax. No sooner had her back touched the seat than another van pulled into the parking lot. She leaned forward again. "That's her." Katía pointed to the first woman out of the van.

"OK. Let her get clocked out, then we'll catch her as she leaves."

When María exited the building, Katía and Luna hopped out of the 4Runner. María's eyes narrowed and darted around the parking lot as they approached.

"Hey, María. This is my friend Luna. Could we talk to you for just a minute?"

"No hablo Inglés."

"Yes, you do." Katía's words came out more aggressively than she had meant.

Luna patted Katía's arm and repeated what she had said in Spanish. Holding out her phone, she showed María a photo of Vitctoria's purse. "She really would like it back. I'll trade you this one for it," she told María in Spanish.

A tear spilled out of María's eye even as she glared at Luna and Katía. "OK." She took the new purse, moved her belongings from Victoria's purse into it, then handed it over.

"Muchas gracias," Luna said.

"Thank you so much. This will mean a lot to my friend. Her daughter made it for her," Katía echoed.

María walked away and sat on a step of the building.

"She looks so sad and frightened," Luna observed. "Does she always seem that way?"

"Now that I think of it, she did seem ill at ease both times I saw her."

"I wonder why."

CHAPTER 12

Friday morning broke crisp and clear. Fitz, Ben, and Zee were already at the park, standing around gabbing, when Katía arrived.

"Mission accomplished," she stated with a big grin.

"You got the purse back?" Ben asked.

"Yep. Luna had a stroke of genius. She brought a new purse and convinced María to swap it for Victoria's. I hope she comes to the park today."

The lights from Luna's 4Runner illuminated the group as she pulled in.

"I don't know," Fitz said. "Yesterday she talked as if that was the last time we'd see her."

"Good morning!" Luna chirped, getting out of her car.

"I hear congratulations are in order," Ben said.

"It was easier than I expected," Luna answered. "Now all we have to do is reunite the purse with its rightful owner."

With jackets zipped and two dogs and a cat leashed up, the group headed down the trail.

"Have y'all ever wondered why we always go the same way?" Zee asked.

"Humans are creatures of habit," Ben laughed. "Besides, there's something about going counterclockwise that's so satisfying."

"I wonder if Speedy'll show up again. I love ogling her car," Zee said.

"We'll have to wait and see," Fitz answered.

They made their way around the trail with no sign of Speedy or Victoria.

"How are we going to get Victoria her purse?" Luna asked.

Katía noted Luna's distress and searched her mind for a solution. "Wait! You know where she lives, Fitz. Didn't you take her home after your heroic deed with the medicine?

"Yeah," Fitz answered.

"Perfect! You can take us to her house," Luna said.

"Do you really think it's a good idea to show up at her house unannounced? Especially this early in the morning," Fitz asked.

Katía flicked her hand toward Fitz. "I'm sure she's up, probably baking conchas."

"I think we should take the purse by," Zee said.

"It'll only take a few minutes. Come on, Fitz," Luna prodded. "I'll drive, and we can all go. It'll be fun to see her reaction."

Katía noticed Fitz digging M&Ms out of his pocket. "You can sit in the front, Fitz."

With the pets stowed in their respective cars, the crew loaded into Luna's 4Runner.

"It's the next driveway," Fitz said, pointing to the left.

Luna turned into the driveway that led to a small, older brick home. A light was on in what appeared to be the kitchen, and Katía could see movement.

"She's going to be so happy to get her purse back," Katía said. She knocked on the door then stepped back. "You should do the honors, Luna."

A preteen girl answered the door in bright blue pajamas with owls.

"Good morning. We're friends of your mom's. Is she here?"

"You have the purse I made! Mamá! These people have your purse!" She left the door open and charged through the house. She came hustling back, tugging Victoria by her hand. "Look, Mamá! They found your purse!"

"Hola," Victoria said, reining the girl to a stop.

"We have a surprise for you," Luna said, holding up the purse.

"¡Gracias a Dios! How did you get it back?"

"We swapped with her."

Victoria and her daughter stepped out onto the little porch. Ben, Zee, and Fitz spilled down the steps. Victoria took the purse and hugged it.

"¡Muchas gracias! I am so happy to have it back. This is mi hija, Sofía." She hugged Sofía, too.

"It's so nice to meet you, Sofía. I hear you're going back to school Monday," Luna said, bending down to the girl's level as she spoke.

"Yeah. I'm ready to see my friends again."

"I'm glad you're looking forward to it. I used to teach high school," Luna said.

"I'll be in high school in three more years," Sofía said.

"I wish I was still working. I might have had you as a student."

"Mamá is starting to work next week."

"You have a precious daughter," Katía said.

"Be careful with your pills. You probably shouldn't carry all of them with you," Fitz instructed.

"I know. I learn my lesson. I only carry the one I need for the day," Victoria answered.

"That's a good idea," Fitz said. "I hope your new job goes well."

Katía noticed Fitz was inching toward the car. "We'll let you get back to it. I trust next week's changes will be good."

The park pals returned to the park and said goodbye till tomorrow.

* * * TWO SATURDAYS LATER * * *

The park pals rounded the curve of the trail closest to the lake. The sun cast an amber glow on the water and sky.

"Looks like God got out the yellow paint today," Zee said.

"It's beautiful," Katía said. "I have to take some pictures." She stopped and set up her camera while the others kept walking.

As they approached the hammock swings, Fitz noticed someone sitting there. "Is that Victoria?"

Her head was bowed. "I think she's prayin'," Zee whispered.

They walked quietly until a squirrel crossed the path and Snickers yelped, tugging at her leash. Victoria looked up and wiped her face.

"Hey, Victoria," Luna said. "How's work going?"

"I made a bad mistake."

"You've been crying. What's wrong?" Luna asked as the group gathered around Victoria.

"I no can say."

"I was afraid it was too early for you to go to work," Luna said. "Is it too hard on you?"

"There are bad people at work. I can no talk about it." Victoria buried her face in her hands. "I need to pray."

CHAPTER 13

The next Tuesday morning the sun was slow to rise, having to work its way through a dense layer of heavy gray clouds. Fitz had finished his morning routine and was sitting in the car with Buffett in his lap waiting for the others.

"They're late this morning, Buffett," Fitz informed the cat.

"Meow."

"Yeah, I'm sure Zee will have treats."

"Meow."

"Is that all you think about?"

"Meow."

Ben pulled up and got out wearing a raincoat, umbrella in hand. "Good morning. It looks like it could come a downpour any time." He leashed up Snickers and let her out of the car.

"It is a dreary day."

"You and Buffett OK?"

"Fine. How about you?"

"I'm good, thanks. I didn't realize how late it was since it stayed so dark."

Buffett and Snickers greeted each other with sniffs. The other three park pals came rolling in one after the other.

"Sorry I'm late," Zee said, trying to hurry out of his car. "These bones just don't move as fast as they used to."

"That's OK. You're worth waiting on," Ben said.

"I was actually talking to Snickers and Buffett. I know they've been expecting me." He produced a biscuit for the tail-wagging dog and treats for Buffett, who was rubbing against his legs. "Yeah, you get one, too," he said, bending down to give King a biscuit. "How is everyone this glorious morning?"

"Fat and sassy," Luna laughed.

"I'll give you the sassy, but I disagree with the fat part," Ben chuckled. "I hope everybody has raingear. We might get a dousing."

Luna and Katía held up umbrellas, and both sported raincoats.

Fitz pulled a brimmed hat over his long salt-and-pepper hair. "I'm set."

"If God wants to give me a shower, I reckon I shouldn't try to get out of it," Zee said, then pointed up the road. "Look what just pulled in! I can't believe she would bring that beautiful car out in the rain."

"Good grief! It's just a car, guys," Luna said.

"No, that's a work of art, like a fine painting," Zee replied.

"We'll have to watch out for her zipping along the trail," Ben said.

Buffett hopped back into Fitz's Highlander. "I don't blame you," Fitz said and unleashed him, leaving him in the car.

The park pals chatted as they made their way around the one-mile trail, having to step aside twice for Speedy to pass.

"How is that parishioner doing, the one where you found Victoria's purse? She had a knee replacement or something," Ben asked.

"She's still hurting but getting better. She keeps taking too many pain pills. She is going to run out of them again."

"That's funny, my aunt did the same thing. She had shoulder surgery about three weeks ago and is going to run out before she sees the surgeon again. I'm sure they won't give her any more," Luna said.

"Helen's surgeon wouldn't prescribe any more for her, either." Katía replied.

About a tenth of a mile from their cars, a gentle rain started to fall.

"Here's my shower for today," Zee quipped as three umbrellas popped open.

"It looks like someone took refuge under the pavilion," Katía noticed as they approached their vehicles.

"I think we should do the same," Ben said.

"Is that Sofía?" Luna asked.

"Sofía?" Ben replied.

"Yeah, Victoria's daughter. Don't you remember?" Luna answered.

"It does look like her," Katía said.

As they got closer, the figure under the pavilion appeared to have noticed them and came running.

"What's wrong, Sofía?" Luna asked when she was close enough to see the distress on her face.

"Mamá didn't come home from work last night. Something bad has happened."

"Oh, no! That's terrible," Luna answered. "Do you have any idea where she might be?"

"No, she just disappeared. We couldn't find her at her office. We looked to see if she was walking home. She was nowhere."

"Did she come back to the office and clock out?" Ben asked.

"I don't know. The office was already closed when we got there."

"Did you call the police?" Luna asked.

"No, Papi said we can't call them since she is illegal." More tears than rain streamed down her face.

Luna wrapped her arm around Sofía. "Come on. Let's get back under the pavilion."

Sofía cried harder. "I was hoping you could help us since you found her purse."

Out of the rain, Luna said, "I'll be happy to do anything I can, and I'm sure my friends will help, too." She looked around to find heads nodding. Fitz stuck his hands in his pockets.

"What can we do to help?" Katía asked.

"I don't know. We just need your help. I want my mamá back."

Luna hugged the girl close. "Fitz, do you have any ideas?"

"Does your mother have a cell phone?"

"Yes. We tried calling, but she didn't answer. It went straight to her voicemail, like the phone was turned off." Sofía answered.

"Do you know her number?" Fitz asked.

"Yes."

"Good. We might be able to locate where she was before it was turned off," Fitz said, looking at Ben with raised eyebrows.

"It's easier to locate a phone that is on, but we can certainly try," Ben responded. "What's her number?" He pulled out his phone, opened a note app, and typed in Victoria's number. "How about your number?" He typed in Sofía's, too. "I'll let you know if I can find anything."

"Thank you so much," Sofía said.

"I'm going to the Sparkles office as soon as I drop you off at your house. I want to find out if they saw anything suspicious," Luna said.

Katía added, "I'll come with you. If we tackle this on two fronts, we'll have a better chance of finding her."

"We'll give you a ride back to the house so you don't get soaked," Luna stated. "We'll do everything we can to find your mother. Ben, let me know as soon as you turn up anything."

"You keep us posted, too," Ben replied.

Luna led Sofía to her car, and she and Katía drove her home. As Sofía hurried toward the house, Katía called out, "I'll keep you in my prayers."

With Katía and Luna gone, Fitz asked, "So do you have any idea how to locate a phone that's been turned off?"

Ben returned a puzzled look. "No, I was hoping you did."

"Man, that's not good," Zee added.

"We sure won't find anything standing here. I need a computer," Ben stated. He started toward the car then looked back. "You coming?"

CHAPTER 14

Fitz nudged Buffett out of his lap after parking on the street in front of Ben's house. "I'll be back. Just enjoy the rain." Zee had pulled in right behind him, and they hustled into the garage before Ben shut the door.

"Ya reckon she's off with a lover?" Zee suggested as the garage door lowered.

"I was wondering the same thing," Fitz said. "But it doesn't seem like she's been here long enough to hook up with another man."

"Sometimes all it takes is one glance," Zee grinned.

Ben added, "She seems like she adores her family. I don't think she's the type to be fooling around."

"True, but that's still the most likely scenario," Fitz said.

Ben led the way into the house. "I'll put on some coffee. I assume everyone has had breakfast."

"I have, thanks, but coffee sounds good," Fitz replied.

"I'm always up for second breakfast," Zee said. "Are you offerin'?"

"I have some cereal," Ben answered.

"That'll do. I haven't had cereal in a long time. Milk's too hard to keep."

Ben set out a bowl, spoon, milk, and his box of granola cereal.

"Thanks," Zee said. "How in the world are you gonna find a cell phone that might not even be on?"

"I have no idea. I hope we can figure something out." He opened the computer to the sound of coffee dripping into the pot.

"There's a website that will locate a phone for a fee, but it has to be on," Fitz offered. "If I were on the force, we could send a signal to ping the phone, but it has to be on. The only evidence I know of for a phone that's off would be the provider records of tower pings. That usually takes a court order."

"That's an idea. Let me find out which carrier she uses." Ben texted Sofía, and she replied instantly

"T-Mobile."

"You know, even if we were to be able to find the last tower the phone pinged, that wouldn't mean anything. She could be anywhere within a fifteen hour drive's radius," Fitz noted.

Ben propped his chin in his hands, elbows resting on the counter. "You're right. I don't think we're going to be able to do anything to help."

"Maybe Luna and Katía will learn something at Sparkles," Fitz replied.

* * * * *

Luna pulled into the Sparkles parking lot. The same burgundy Camry was parked in Shannon's spot. A green Hummer was parked three spaces down. A white Corvette was parked next to the Camry. The sign in front of it read, "Crystal."

"Is that the same car Zee and Fitz have been drooling over?" Katía asked.

"It sure looks like it. Maybe Speedy works here."

"With a car like that, I'd say she probably owns the place."

"There's only one way to find out. Let's go," Luna said.

Katía got out and wiped her sweaty palms on her slacks. *Why am I nervous?*

"Are you sure you're up for this?" Luna asked.

"It shows, huh? Yeah, I'm up for it. I just have an odd feeling about it."

As they climbed the steps, the front door opened and a huge man exited. He must have been six feet four. Thick, with muscles bulging under his black leather jacket. His jet black hair was pulled into a pony tail, and he sported a goatee. The rest of his outfit consisted of black jeans and a white polo.

He glanced at Katía, and his piercing dark, mean eyes sent a chill down her spine. He continued on to the Hummer without a word.

"That guy was scary," Katía whispered.

"I thought he was good looking," Luna whispered back, opening the door and stepping in. She paused holding the door for Katía. "Come on."

Katía's shoes felt glued to the landing. With effort, she managed to move through the door and follow Luna.

To the right was a room with lockers and benches. A door on the left afforded a view of a room packed with cleaning supplies. There was a stairway with a sign that read, "OFFICES" and an arrow pointing up.

"It looks like we go upstairs," Luna said as she started to climb.

Katía followed, trying to shake her unease. *We're just asking about Victoria. There's nothing to worry about. I just freaked out when I saw that man. I guess he reminded me of the Confederate Rising gang.* Katía still had flashbacks to the time she was held captive by that gang. She wondered if she would ever get fully over the incident.

The stairs ended on a landing with two doors, each with a sign. One read, "Shannon Bledsoe, Office Manager." The other sign was larger and bolder: "Crystal Samson."

"It's Speedy," Luna whispered, having spotted the woman through the window in the door.

"It's a small world," Katía replied.

Luna knocked on the door, and the woman looked up from her desk with a puzzled expression. She waved them in.

"Hi, I'm Luna, and this is Katía."

"It's nice to meet you. I'm Crystal Samson. What can I do for you? If you're looking for a cleaning service, you've come to the right place."

"A friend of ours went missing last night, and we're trying to find her.

"I'm sorry to hear that, but I don't know of anyone who is missing," Crystal replied.

"She works for Sparkles. Her name is Victoria López, and we wondered if she clocked out yesterday. That could help us pin down when she disappeared," Luna explained.

"That's not something I keep up with, but Shannon could help." Crystal hit the intercom button on the phone. "Shannon, did Victoria López clock out yesterday?"

"Just a second."

Katía looked across the hall and could see Shannon clicking the mouse for her computer.

"She clocked out at four forty-seven."

"Thank you, Shannon," Crystal replied. "As you hear, she did clock out yesterday, so it had to have happened after she left here. If there's nothing else, I need to get back to work."

"Thanks for your help," Luna said, turning to leave.

"Do you have security cameras? Could we check to see if someone grabbed her in the parking lot?" Katía asked.

Crystal's eyes turned dagger-like. "I can assure you no one was abducted in our parking lot, but if you'll wait downstairs, I'll ask Shannon to check the footage." Crystal rounded the desk and opened the door, signaling for them to leave.

Katía sensed Crystal's anger as she passed. She and Luna walked down the stairs to wait.

"That was odd," Katía whispered.

"I get the sense she's not a pleasant woman," Luna said.

After a couple of minutes, footsteps on the stairs announced Shannon's coming.

"I'm sorry for the disappearance of your friend. Our security system showed her getting into a car like she usually does. It was probably an Uber or Lyft," she explained. Shannon was forty-ish with brown shoulder-length hair and glasses. "I hope you are able to find her. Oh, she didn't clock in this morning, if that helps."

Shannon turned and climbed the stairs, leaving Katía and Luna to process what she had said.

CHAPTER 15

Katía held the door for Luna as they exited the Sparkles building, feeling perplexed. Two ideas were tumbling around in her mind. *She could be cheating on her husband and is off with another man. The driver could have abducted her.* Neither thought was pleasant. Luna apparently noticed the trouble etched on her face.

"What's eating at you?" Luna asked.

"I can think of two possibilities for Luna's disappearance, and neither is good."

"Let's get into the car before you tell me."

With the car doors closed, Katía proceeded to explain. "She could have run off with another man, or the driver that picked her up could have abducted her and left her dead somewhere when he was through with her."

"You're right. Those are bad scenarios. I can think of a third. What if Crystal and Shannon were lying?"

Katía's face scrunched up. "Why would they lie?"

"I just have an uneasy feeling about them. What if they were behind her disappearance?"

"I can't imagine why an employer would abduct their own employee. I get what you're saying about something being off with them, though. They were a bit... curt."

"I just hope they can't read our lips from their video footage." Luna cranked the car and took off out of the parking lot. They rode in silence, pondering the implications of their thoughts.

Luna sighed, then said, "OK, now what can we do?"

"I wonder if Uber would tell us if a driver picked up Victoria yesterday."

"I doubt it, but it's worth a try," Luna responded.

Katía slid her phone from her purse and did a search for Uber. She scanned the website. "I don't see any contact information." Tapping on the "About Us" button, she still found no way to contact them.

"Maybe there's a contact number listed where you apply for jobs," Luna suggested.

After scanning that page, Katía said, "Nope. I can fill out the application form or connect on Linkedin."

"Try searching for Uber's phone number."

Katía typed that in, having to correct twice because the car hit bumps. "This looks promising." She tapped one of the search responses. "Get this. It gives a number, then says, 'This number isn't guaranteed to provide an Uber support representative.' Wait, there's a number for emergencies, too."

Luna looked over. "I'd say this is an emergency. Try it and see what happens.

Katía placed the call and waited. When a woman answered, she explained the situation. "Is there any way you can tell me if she was picked up by one of your drivers? Her name is Victoria López… Well, thanks anyway."

"Nothing?"

"No, she said they aren't permitted to give out that information." Katía jammed the phone back into her purse.

"I wonder if they would be more cooperative if the police called."

Katía eyed Luna. "You're not thinking what I think you're thinking, are you?"

"Maybe," Luna answered, a slight grin forming.

"You do realize it's illegal to impersonate an officer, right?"

"True, but how else are we going to find out?"

Katía scrunched up her eyes, trying to read Luna's face. "Let's talk to Fitz and Ben before we do anything crazy. I should get to the office, but this is more important."

Luna pulled in behind Fitz's and Zee's cars in front of Ben's house. "I hope they've had more luck than we have."

"I've got it," Katía heard Zee call after she rang the doorbell.

Snickers and King greeted Katía and Luna as they entered with tail wags and licks.

"I hope y'all had better luck than we did," Katía said.

"You'll never guess who we talked to," Luna added.

"You're right. I won't guess," Fitz grumped.

"Speedy is the owner of Sparkles," Luna said as they all gathered in the den.

"Did you ask her for a ride in the car?" Zee asked.

"No, we didn't," Katía shook her head. "Her assistant said that their security video showed Victoria getting into a car after work yesterday. She assumed it was a Lyft or Uber. Were y'all able to find her phone?" she asked, scanning the three men's faces.

"No. We realized there is nothing we can do with a phone that's not on," Ben said.

Katía's heart dropped. "What else can we do?"

"Let's list some options," Luna said. "What are some possible scenarios?"

"She could have run off with another man," Zee offered.

"We wondered if the driver who picked her up abducted her," Luna said.

"I think the driver abducting her is the most likely scenario," Fitz added. "She doesn't seem like the type to have abandoned her family out of lust."

"We tried calling Uber, and they wouldn't tell us if one of their drivers picked her up," Katía said.

"Did you tell them she was missing?" Ben asked.

"Of course. They just said they can't give out that information," Katía added.

Ben summed up the situation. "So her last known location was the Sparkles parking lot after work yesterday. Someone picked her up, and she hasn't been seen since. I think our next step is to find out who picked her up."

"We could try talking to some of the workers as they come in this afternoon. They might have seen the car she got into," Luna suggested.

"That gives the abductor a long head start, but it's the best option I see right now," Fitz said.

Ben slammed his hand onto his thigh. "I should have thought of this before. What if one of the traffic cameras can see the Sparkles parking lot?"

CHAPTER 16

Victoria slumped against the wall, head in her hands, tears streaming. Light seeped through the cracks in the wall of the shed, but it was still dark. She could barely make out some of the things stored in there, like a couple of saddles and a huge lawnmower.

She had tried kicking the door and ramming her shoulder into it. It held tight. Her shoulder didn't. It hurt. She had searched for something with which to break through the door but had found nothing. The key wasn't even in the lawnmower. Given the temperament of the man who abducted her, she wasn't surprised that there was no way to escape.

She sat worrying and crying. She had only one more immunosuppressant pill. She had no way to contact her family. *What is going to happen to me? I miss mi hija. Mi esposo. What can I do?*

It was thinking of her family that had her crying at this moment. She feared she would never see them again, never get to say goodbye.

She had yelled for help till her throat hurt. No one came. The light was slowly fading. Night was coming. Soon she would be in total darkness.

What worried her the most was her captor's last words. "You should be deported, but it's quicker and easier to kill you."

CHAPTER 17

en rushed to the computer after realizing he could check traffic cameras to see if they could identify whom Victoria rode off with. Luna, Katía, Fitz, and Zee hovered around him.

"Do you remember how you got in last time?" Fitz asked.

Ben looked up with a scowl. "Of course I remember." He pulled up the Sparkles address and copied it. A few minutes later he was into the system and pulling up cameras. "The closest one is at Hilton and Atlanta Highway. What time do they get off?"

Luna answered, "I think Speedy said it was four forty-seven when Luna clocked out, didn't she?" She looked to Katía for confirmation. Katía nodded.

Ben pulled up the footage starting at four o'clock yesterday afternoon and set it to scroll through the images quickly. When they saw the first Sparkles van go by, he slowed it down.

"This should be the route an Uber driver would go to take Victoria home. It would be farther to go out Hilton Drive to Browns Bridge," Fitz noted.

Ben paused the footage for each car that pulled up to the traffic light on Hilton Drive. After pausing for the third car, he said, "I don't think this is going to help since we can't see anyone in the back seat, and I suspect that's where Victoria would be."

"She might sit in the front," Luna said. "She seems friendly."

"OK, I'll keep going," Ben said with no enthusiasm. They kept searching till the time stamp said five thirty.

Katía stretched. "My neck's sore, and it's been a long time since we've seen a Sparkles van."

The others joined in stretching and groaning.

"You're right. I think she would be gone by now," Fitz said.

"Of course, if an abductor picked her up, he might have driven the other way on Hilton, depending on where he was taking her," Luna noted.

"He also might have insisted she sit in the back, where he had the child locks on so she couldn't jump out," Ben added.

Fitz popped three M&Ms into his mouth.

"What's wrong, Fitz?" Katía asked.

Fitz tensed, realizing he had been caught. He considered lying but decided to share his thoughts. "I'm afraid the most likely scenario in this case is rape and murder. We're probably too late to help."

Luna's hands landed on her hips with resolve. "Well, I'm not giving up. Victoria's life is worth doing everything we can. We need more ideas. What else can we do?"

Fitz dug into his brain, searching for ideas. He checked the clock. It was 10:07. Ben's getting up and stating he would put on more coffee barely registered. *How can we possibly find her? It's like hunting a needle in a haystack, and we're wearing sunglasses.*

"What if we go around town and put up fliers with her picture on it?" Katía asked.

"That would take too much time," Fitz replied. "Besides, if she's still alive, she'll be held in a place no one can see her." He went back to his thoughts with another round of M&Ms. *When we lost Katía, at least we knew who we were hunting. Now we have no idea. When there's no way forward, we have to go with our hunches.*

"Does anyone have any suspicions, even just a hunch as to what might have happened?" he asked.

"I'm suspicious of Sparkles. Something is just not quite right there. Plus, a man came out of there who gave me the creeps," Katía stated.

"What about him gave you the creeps?" Fitz asked.

"His eyes seemed mean," Katía answered. "I think he reminded me of the gang members who held me captive."

Fitz paused, then said, "I recommend we concentrate on Sparkles then. That's really all we have."

"But the office manager said Victoria left in a car," Luna said.

"Did you see the video of that?" Fitz asked.

"No."

"Could she have been lying?" Fitz asked.

"That's possible," Luna replied.

"Why would an employer kidnap their own employee?" Ben asked.

"I don't know, but we need to find out," Fitz said. "Could she have been held in the Sparkles building?"

"I don't think so. It's not that large, and I didn't hear anyone yelling or banging," Luna answered.

"She might have given up by then," Zee observed.

"Did you notice any outbuildings?" Fitz asked.

"Not that I remember," Katía said.

Back at the computer, Ben said, "This might help." He had pulled up the Sparkles building on the map and zoomed in.

The park pals gathered around Ben. "No outbuildings," he said.

"If they have her, then they must be holding her somewhere else," Luna said.

"Tell me again why we're assuming Sparkles is behind this," Ben said.

"Because Katía's hunch is all we have," Fitz answered. "We need to pay another visit to Sparkles."

"If they lied to us once, I don't think they'll be forthcoming the second time," Luna said. "Speedy was quite curt, though. It makes me wonder."

Katía put her hand to her chin. "The workers might be willing to talk, though. We could show up and ask if they saw anything."

"You're right," Fitz stated. "Let's show up at Sparkles at four o'clock. We'll definitely need Luna since some of them might not speak English."

CHAPTER 18

Fitz lingered as the others left with the plan to meet at Sparkles at four o'clock to interview the workers.

"I won't be able to make it, but I'll see y'all in the mornin'," Zee said as he walked out the door.

"If you don't have plans, we need to learn everything we can about the Sparkles owner before we go out there," Fitz said to Ben.

"Bummer. I thought you were going to suggest we do something fun. Sure, I have time. Want another cup of coffee?"

"That would be great." Fitz sat at the counter on a bar stool and opened his phone, but his mind was on what Ben had said. *Maybe we could do something fun together one day. What would that be?*

Ben set two mugs on the counter and brought over his computer. "What did they say Speedy's real name was?"

"I don't believe they said."

"I'm sure I can find it on the website," Ben said as he pulled up Sparklescleaning.com. "Crystal Samson is our person of interest."

"If I were still on the force, the first thing I would do is check to see if she has any prior arrests."

Ben was studying the computer screen. On his phone, Fitz opened the Sparkles website to find Crystal front and center with the company logo below.

"It looks like someone has an ego," Fitz said.

"I guess she considers herself the face of Sparkles."

While Ben looked over the Sparkles website, Fitz went back and did a search for "Crystal Samson Gainesville GA."

"It looks like she's a philanthropist. There are a couple of articles about donations she has made," Fitz noted. He continued scanning. "Here's one about her divorce. Hmm, her ex is a lawyer with the DA's office, Darryl Samson."

"I've heard of him. It looks like we're dealing with the high society of Hall County. I'm not finding much of interest on this website. She mostly touts how she grew Sparkles into a thriving business… Wait, here is a link to a wedding venue she owns."

He followed the link. "Pretty. It has a nice view of the mountains. A couple of horses, too. It's up in Clermont. I don't think she looks like the criminal type."

"Looks can be deceiving," Fitz replied. "I doubt she would list any criminal activity on her websites."

"I realize that, but if she's a philanthropist and successful business woman, why would she need to abduct a Latina woman?"

"I have no idea. We might be barking up the wrong tree, but let's keep barking." Fitz scrolled through a few more articles on Crystal Samson before noticing the newspaper lying on the counter. "You have a subscription to the paper."

"Yeah, I thought you knew that."

"Can you access the online content?"

"Yeah."

"Try pulling it up and searching the archives. There might be something helpful there." Fitz suddenly felt hopeful. *Maybe this is going to turn into more than just something to do since there were no other options.*

Ben logged into his account with the Times. "What am I looking for?"

"I have no idea. Just search the archives for Crystal Samson and then Sparkles." He headed toward the coffee pot. "Want another cup?"

"No, thanks. I've hit my caffeine ceiling."

"I didn't know there was such a thing," Fitz said, pouring himself another cup.

"Yeah, too much makes me jumpy."

Fitz looked over Ben's shoulder. He was scrolling through the same articles Fitz had already scanned. "Other than her divorce, she looks squeaky clean."

Ben searched for Sparkles, and Fitz sat back down. *It has to be the driver who picked her up … unless they were lying.*

"That looks serious," Ben said.

"Did you find something?"

"No, I mean your face. What are you pondering?"

"The thought that they could have been lying about Victoria getting picked up crossed my mind."

"I suppose that's possible," Ben replied.

"You don't sound convinced."

"I still think your original theory about a taxi driver picking her up and abducting her is more likely."

"But wouldn't the ride share companies know the rider wasn't delivered to the correct address?" Fitz asked.

"They wouldn't if the driver drove by her home first. It would look like the creep had taken her there," Ben observed.

Fitz stood up. "I wonder if Sofía noticed a car pull in the driveway. We need to give her an update anyway." He started pacing. After turning and coming back, he stopped. "Well?"

"Oh, you want me to talk to her," Ben said. He pulled out his phone and placed the call. Sofía answered on the first ring.

Ben said, "Hey, Sofía. I'm sorry to say that we haven't turned up anything on your mother yet. We were wondering if you noticed a car pull into your driveway or go past the house slowly yesterday about the time your mother should have come home."

Fitz could tell from Ben's expression that Sofía's answer was, "No."

"We thought that if an Uber or Lyft driver abducted her they might have come to your house to make it look like they dropped her off. We'll be sure to let you know if we find anything. In the meantime, feel free to call if you want to. … Bye."

Ben looked to Fitz, "That wasn't a bit of fun. I feel sorry for Sofía. She has to be hurting."

"I'm sure. Call her back."

"Why?"

"Let's find out if she always used the same rideshare company," Fitz said.

"Why didn't we think of that sooner?" Ben called and Sofía told them that she usually used Uber, unless they were too busy for a quick pick up.

Fitz waved his arms. "Tell her to call Uber and report that her mother is missing after being picked up by one of their drivers."

"Did you hear that?" Ben asked Sofía.

"Hold on a minute, and I'll find the number." Fitz held out his phone with the Uber site pulled up, and Ben relayed the number.

"Please let us know what they say," Ben said before disconnecting.

Fitz sat back down with his coffee, and Ben returned to searching the paper's archives.

"Well, look at this. I finally found some dirt on Sparkles."

"What is it?" Fitz asked, coming to see the screen.

"It looks like one of Sparkles' employees was indicted for stealing opioids from a client's home," Ben answered.

Fitz leaned in to discover he couldn't read anything but the headline. "I can't see it. You'll have to tell me what you find," he said, straightening up.

"Nope. No dirt. It says the employee was cleared of all charges. Sparkles remains untarnished."

Ben's phone rang. "It's Sofía."

Ben answered and listened. "I'm sorry. That's the same thing they told Katía when she called. I was hoping they would talk to you since you're family. We'll stay in touch."

"No luck?" Fitz asked.

"No. They told her to file a report with the police," Ben said, shaking his head.

Fitz tugged his beard. "It's not looking good."

CHAPTER 19

Fitz was surprised when he realized he wasn't in a rush to leave Ben's house. Normally, he would have been itching to get back to his car where he could be alone with Buffett. It was 11:04, and they had exhausted ideas for internet searches.

"Would you like to stay for lunch?" Ben asked. "I have plenty of stuff for sandwiches."

Fitz started to give his automatic response of, "No, I need to get going." Instead he paused. "That would be nice. Thank you," he answered. Without even realizing it, he popped three M&Ms into his mouth. He immersed himself back into trying to figure out how to find Victoria.

"I see what you're thinking, but I don't know of anything else we can do till we go out to Sparkles," Ben said.

"There's always something else to be done. There's something we're missing."

"Like Luna said, we could put fliers up with her picture on it," Ben suggested.

"I don't think that would do any good, but a picture would be helpful. Let's see if Sofía has a picture of her."

"OK. I hate bothering her again."

"If my mother were missing, I wouldn't consider it a bother."

"True." Ben texted Sofía and asked if she had a photo they could use. Her response came quickly with a close-up photo of Victoria and Sofía. "Thanks," Ben replied. He held up the photo for Fitz to see.

"Perfect. Do you have a printer? We might need to show the workers what she looks like."

"Why don't I just text the photo to everyone, and we can show them on our phones?"

"I guess that'll work, too," Fitz replied.

"If you like, you're welcome to a shower before lunch," Ben offered.

Fitz's initial impulse was to turn down the idea, but the thought of the warm water splashing onto his body was too tempting. "That would be wonderful," he answered. "Let me get some clean clothes from the car."

Fitz slid into the driver's seat and explained what was going on to Buffett, who had been sleeping in the sun since the sky had cleared. He slipped Buffett a few treats. "Thanks for being patient. You're such a good cat."

"Meow."

Fitz emerged from the shower all warm and clean. "That was nice. Thank you."

"You're quite welcome," Ben replied as he set lunch items onto the table. "I texted everyone Victoria's picture. I have ham, turkey, lettuce, tomato, and pickles. I hope that will do."

"That works for me," Fitz answered.

"Come on, Snickers. It's time for you to go out," Ben said, opening the back door. Snickers trotted out.

While Snickers was out romping in the yard, Ben and Fitz sat down to lunch. With sandwiches prepared, Ben asked, "How long have you lived in your car?"

Fitz quickly took a bite of sandwich to give himself time to ready his response. After swallowing, he said, "I guess it's been about four years now."

"Wow. That's a long time."

"It seems to be working. Buffett and I are happy together."

They ate in silence for a while, which suited Fitz just fine.

"Were you ever married?" Ben asked.

That hit a nerve, and Fitz stiffened. He didn't want to go there. Bringing up memories of Sharon, the love of his life with whom he would rendezvous when they were on leave in the army, was just too hard and not something he wanted to do with someone around. Ben apparently noticed.

"I'm sorry. It's OK if you don't want to answer that."

I stayed for lunch. Isn't that enough? I just can't talk about Sharon. Fitz wiped his mouth and breathed. "No, I wasn't married. Maybe we should be talking about how to find Victoria."

"OK. I was just chatting. You're an interesting fellow, and I wanted to learn more about you. Can you think of anything to do besides going to talk with the workers with regard to finding Victoria?"

"Not without involving the police. Alerting the public to be on the lookout for her would be worthless. Whoever took her has her hidden if she's not already dead."

"Do you think we're wasting our time trying to find her. Is there any hope?"

"It's never a waste of time to try to rescue someone from death. There are other scenarios besides abduction, rape, then murder."

Ben finished chewing and swallowed. "Like what?"

Fitz stroked his long salt and pepper beard. "Let's see, ransom, sex worker, forced drug smuggling, forced domestic worker, just to name a few."

"I don't think she fits into the usual sex worker profile and kidnapping her for ransom seems pointless," Ben replied.

"True. But she would make an ideal drug smuggler. No one would suspect her."

"I see what you're saying," Ben said, then took a drink of iced tea. "If that's the case, at least she would still be alive."

"But would they keep her in this area? They might hold her somewhere till they had broken her enough that she's willing to do whatever they tell her."

Ben scowled. "That doesn't sound good."

"At least she would still be alive, if that's the case."

"And we might have a chance to find her."

Snickers barked, and Ben got up to let her in. Sitting back down he asked, "Do you think Sparkles could be connected with drug smuggling in some way?"

"I have no idea. Like you said, it looks squeaky clean from what we've seen so far."

Fitz took the last bite of his sandwich and drifted off into thought. *The drug business changes quickly. I wonder if any of the dealers I used to know are still around. I wonder if I can remember who they are. Even if I could, how would I contact them? Oh, yeah. Gizmo. I remember him, and I know where to find him.*

"A penny for your thoughts," Ben said, dragging Fitz back.

"I was just remembering a drug dealer I used to know and wondering if he could tell us anything."

"Great! Can we see him before four o'clock?"

"I had better go alone. It could be dangerous."

Ben rolled his eyes. "I'm not worried about danger. And if it's going to be dangerous, it would be better if there were two of us."

Fitz couldn't think of an argument against what Ben had said, so he agreed to Ben coming along.

CHAPTER 20

Fitz directed Ben to some apartments on Old Athens Road. They parked in a lot with a sidewalk leading to the apartment where Fitz remembered Gizmo lived.

"I hope he still lives here," Fitz said.

"How long ago was it that you knew he lived here?" Ben asked.

"Maybe five years."

"Fitz, what makes you think a drug dealer would live in the same place that long?"

"Gizmo's a homebody. He's not much for change."

The apartment door opened and three men walked out.

"That looks promising," Fitz said.

"You mean you think those guys just bought drugs from him?"

"It's more likely he just furnished them a supply to sell, and they'll have to pay him before they can get more."

"Oh. Now I see why you said this might be dangerous."

Fitz eyed Ben but didn't see any signs of fear. He asked anyway. "Do you want to stay in the car?"

"What? No way am I missing meeting this character."

They walked up to the door, and Fitz knocked. There was no response.

Fitz knocked again and said, "It's Fitz."

The door cracked open. "What do you want, Fitz? And who's the goon with you?"

"He's a friend. I just have a couple of questions for you."

"Hurry up before someone sees you." Gizmo opened the door wider and stepped back. "I don't want you damagin' my reputation."

"I thought you were out of police work," Gizmo said when they were inside. "Sit down. Get comfortable. Can I get you something to drink?"

"No, thanks," Fitz said. "You're right, I'm no longer in police work. A friend of ours has been abducted."

"That's bad. You know I don't do stuff like that. I'm legit."

"I know you wouldn't abduct someone and force them to smuggle."

"Why you here then?"

"I hoped you might know someone who is doing that," Fitz answered.

"Doin' what?"

"Forcing people to be mules and smuggle drugs into the country." Fitz said, trying to keep the irritation out of his voice.

"Naw, man. I wouldn't know nothin' about that stuff."

"You have to get your supply from somewhere. How do they get it here?" Fitz knew he was pushing but hoped Gizmo wouldn't clam up.

"Now you askin' for trade secrets. As far as I know my man don't do that crap. Of course, I ain't asked him how he gets his goods."

"How about anybody else's suppliers? Any of your pals have suppliers using forced mules?" Fitz asked.

"Man, I don't know anyone doin' that bad stuff."

Fitz knew that's all he would get from Gizmo. He pulled a card from his pocket. "You got a pen?"

Gizmo handed over a pen, and Fitz wrote his number on the card. "If you hear anything, please let me know. Her life depends on it."

"For sure. I ain't about anybody bein' forced to do nothin'."

"Thanks. It's good to see you again," Fitz said and turned toward the door. "Oh, if you get a chance, ask around."

"You all right, Fitz. I'll keep an ear out."

"It was nice to meet you," Ben added.

"Any friend of Fitz's is a friend of mine," Gizmo said.

Gizmo closed the door behind them, and they walked to the car.

"That was interesting," Ben said, closing the car door.

"How so?"

"He, being a drug dealer, seemed to like you even though you're a cop."

"Are you saying I'm not likeable?" Fitz countered.

"Not at all. It just seems like an odd friendship."

"We go way back, and I try to be nice to him so he's more willing to help out when I need him."

As they were pulling out of the apartment complex, Ben asked, "Do you believe him?"

"Actually, I do. I can picture Gizmo picking up his supply and not asking any questions. It's probably safer that way."

"So we don't know any more than before we talked to him."

"We know that Gizmo doesn't know who abducted her. That's something," Fitz answered. He checked his watch. It was 2:03pm, two hours till they were to meet at Sparkles. *I should have brought my car. What am I going to do for two hours?* He dug M&Ms out of his pocket.

"Hey, why don't we try one of the coffee shops on the square? We have about two hours to kill, and I don't see any point in driving all the way back to the house. It's my treat."

Fitz relaxed a bit. "That sounds good."

They parked in the parking deck and found a coffee shop on Bradford Street not far from where they exited the deck.

Fitz ordered a cappuccino, and Ben had a cold brew.

Looking out the window, Fitz said, "I'm glad the clouds are back so I don't have to worry about Buffett getting too hot. Even on a cool day like this the sun can warm up the car."

"I thought Buffett likes it hot."

"He does, but I don't want it to get too hot on him."

Ben hopped up to get their order. When he sat back down, he asked, "Any other ideas for how we could get a lead on Victoria come to mind?"

"I was just pondering that. So far I've got nothing."

"Hey, remember that reporter at the Times who helped us out last time?"

"Yeah. Serena."

"Maybe they've covered a story on this issue."

Fitz took a sip of his coffee. "This is good. Let me give her a call." He called and asked for Serena.

"Hey, Fitz! Let me guess. You're in trouble again."

"What makes you think that?" Fitz asked.

"Why else would you call?"

"Actually you're right. Well, it's a friend who's in trouble. A woman has been abducted."

"Oh, no. That's terrible."

"I was wondering if the paper has covered any stories about drug suppliers in the area using mules to smuggle in their supplies."

There was a pause. Apparently Serena was thinking. "I don't recall anything like that, but I'll be happy to search our archives and get back to you."

"Thanks. This woman's life might depend on it," Fitz said.

He summed up the conversation for Ben, who held up crossed fingers. "I hope she finds something."

CHAPTER 21

Ben and Fitz pulled into the Sparkles parking lot at 3:55pm. Luna and Katía were already there and sitting in Luna's car.

"It looks like the ambush is set," Ben chuckled as he and Fitz walked up to Luna's car.

"We wanted to get here a little early just in case one of the vans got here sooner than we expected," Luna said.

"I wonder how management is going to feel about our interrogating their workers," Fitz said.

"I hadn't thought about that," Katía responded. She stepped out of the car. A light breeze blew, and she folded her arms with a shiver, wishing she had a jacket.

Fitz's phone rang, and he answered Serena's call. Disconnecting, he reported to the gang that she had found nothing on drug smugglers.

"Does everyone have Victoria's picture pulled up?" Ben asked.

"Oh, yeah," Fitz said and opened the text to pull up the photo.

A van pulled into the parking lot, and four women got out.

"It looks like it's one apiece. Let's see what they have to say," Luna said.

"I'll take María," Katía said and headed her direction. The others fanned out to corral the other three women.

"Hey, María. It's Katía."

"Yeah, I remember you."

"I hope you're enjoying the purse Luna got for you."

"I am."

"Listen, do you know Victoria?" Katía held up the photo? She was tense with expectation.

"I don't know her, but I saw her once at our weekly meeting. She must not have liked the job because I haven't seen her since."

"She disappeared yesterday after clocking out. I was hoping you might have seen her leave, maybe have noticed what type of car she got into."

María's eyes widened, and she stiffened. "Like I said, I haven't seen her since last Wednesday."

Katía heard the building door open and glanced over. Shannon, the office manager, emerged with fire in her eyes. "What, may I ask, are you people doing?" she said as she marched up to Katía.

"We're asking the workers if anyone saw the car Victoria got into yesterday after work. If anyone can describe it, that might help us find her," Katía answered, squaring off as if ready for a fight.

Shannon had to look up, and her face softened. "That does make sense. I apologize if I came on strong. We're very protective of our employees."

Shannon turned and called out, "Girls, one of our employees, Victoria, seems to have gone missing after work yesterday. These people are trying to help find her. If anyone saw the car she got into, let them know." She repeated it in Spanish.

She turned to Katía. "Actually, I can give you a description of the car since we have it on tape. I'll be right back. You might ask if they can describe the driver." Shannon scurried back into the building.

Katía looked to María, and she shook her head. "I didn't even see Victoria, much less the driver. I need to clock out. They don't like it if we linger. They think we're trying to pad our time."

When María came back out, she bumped into Katía as she walked past and slipped her a note. "Don't look at that yet." She whispered and walked on.

Katía's eyes widened. She sensed that she needed to hide the note and quickly slid it into her pocket. It took a lot of will power not to pull it out and read it.

Another van pulled in, and the park pals started showing the workers Victoria's picture and asking if anyone could describe the driver of the vehicle she left in.

After a few minutes, Shannon returned with a piece of paper. "The car was a white Toyota Corolla. Four doors. I couldn't get the tag number because another car was right behind it." She handed Katía the piece of paper on which she had written the car's description.

"Could you tell if the car was an Uber or Lyft?" Katía asked.

"No, I didn't see any signs on it. You're welcome to question more of the workers." Shannon turned and went back into the building.

Four more vans dropped off workers. Most of the ones they tried to question responded with, "No hablo Inglés." Luna was the only one who succeeded with communicating, and still, the workers seemed reluctant even to tell her they had not seen anything.

Luna, Fitz, Ben and Katía gathered beside Luna's car. "I get the feeling they don't want to talk to us," Ben said.

"You can say that again," Katía agreed.

"I'm betting most of them are undocumented and are leery of strangers asking questions," Fitz pointed out.

"Still, they seemed to be hiding something," Katía replied.

Luna nodded. "I agree. They seemed more anxious than just wanting to keep their legal status hidden, especially since all we were asking was to help find one of their coworkers."

Katía said, "I don't want to pull it out since they are probably watching us on the cameras, but María slipped me a note when she came out after clocking out."

"Wow! I can't wait to see what it says," Luna said. "But you're right. Don't pull it out here."

"Do you know where the Atlanta Street Seafood Market is?" Ben asked. "We could meet there to see what the note says."

"Yeah, that's a great idea." Luna answered. "We'll see you there." Luna was hopping into the car before the others had processed what she said. She stuck her head back out. "Come on! Let's go!"

As soon as they were down the road from the Sparkles parking lot, Katía pulled the note from her pocket. "It's in Spanish."

"I can read it at the traffic light," Luna said. "Oops, I guess not." The light turned green as they approached.

When they parked, Luna took the note. "Meet me at J and J's parking lot in twenty minutes." Luna looked at her watch. "How long ago did she give it to you?"

"I don't know, I didn't check my watch. It's probably been at least twenty minutes, though."

Ben and Fitz pulled in beside them. Luna rolled down her window. "Come on. We have to get to J and J's." Without any further explanation, she backed out and took off for the grocery store, which was just up the road.

Katía scanned the parking lot as Luna flew into it. "I don't see her!" Her nerves got even tighter. "What if we missed her?"

"Don't panic. She's probably inside the store. I bet she came here to buy groceries before going home," Luna said as she pulled into a parking place.

Katía opened the door before the car fully stopped. "You wait out here and I'll check the store." She took off at a trot.

Ben parked next to Luna, and he and Fitz got out. "What's the rush?" Ben asked.

"The note told us to meet María here in twenty minutes. I hope we didn't miss her. Katía's checking inside."

"She wanted to tell us something, and she didn't want her boss to know she was talking to us," Fitz mused.

Katía squelched the desire to run and walked quickly, looking down each aisle. She hadn't seen María by the time she reached the end of the store, so she doubled back, checking more carefully. Katía almost missed seeing her turn down the aisle with the canned vegetables. She put on the brakes and turned down the aisle to meet María.

"Hey. I was afraid we had missed you. I didn't want to look at the note while we were within sight of the cameras, and it was over twenty minutes before we read it," Katía explained in a rush. She realized she had worked herself into a sweat.

"It's OK. We talk outside, though," María responded.

"Sure. That's fine. Do you want me to wait outside or walk with you?"

"I'm almost through," María said.

Katía sensed that María wanted her to wait outside, so she said, "OK, we'll be in the parking lot." Katía walked back outside in less of a panic.

"She's finishing up her grocery shopping and will talk to us out here," Katía explained to the other park pals.

CHAPTER 22

Ben eyed the store, waiting for María to come out. "It looks like your hunch was right on the money, Katía." It was nearly five o'clock, and the breeze was getting cooler.

"I still can't imagine why the Sparkles folks would kidnap one of their workers," Ben continued. "It just doesn't make sense."

"Let's not jump to conclusions. We don't know what María wants to tell us. It might not have anything to do with Victoria," Fitz said.

Fitz could tell from the others' expressions that they didn't believe him. The awkward moment was relieved when María walked out the door.

She carried groceries in three bags, and her face held a somber expression.

"I hope she doesn't back out of telling us," Fitz muttered. He had seen that look before and sensed that what María had to say was important and dangerous. A palpable silence gripped everyone as María joined the group.

"I don't know if I can do this," María said and started to turn away.

"Wait. We will keep whatever you tell us a secret," Luna said.

María turned back, her eyes pleading. "Please promise you will never tell where you got this information."

"We promise," Katía said, and the others nodded.

"The Sparkles lady…"

"What about her," Fitz encouraged during María's pause.

"She… makes us steal pain pills from clients. She says she will deport us if we don't or if we tell anyone. I think she will just kill us instead of deporting us. She's a bad woman."

"Is that what happened to Victoria?" Luna asked.

"I don't know, but probably. She was new and might not have wanted to steal once she found out what was expected. Crystal wouldn't have let her quit."

"Do you really think she would kill Victoria for that?" Ben asked, eyes wide.

"I think she is a bad person. I don't want to steal, either, but I have no choice. I have to go. I shouldn't have told you this." María turned and started to walk away.

"Wait," Luna called. "I'll be happy to give you a ride home."

María stopped and slowly turned around. "I would be grateful. It would save me money."

With the groceries and María loaded into the car, Luna and Katía drove off, leaving Ben and Fitz in the parking lot.

"Are you thinking what I'm thinking?" Ben asked.

"Probably. We need to check out Samson's wedding venue."

Ben was already searching for the address.

They started heading north on Hwy. 129. Fitz said, "I think we need to stop by your house for my gun."

"Good idea. I can let Snickers out, too."

"I'll get out one of my extras for you."

"That's OK, I'll use my own Glock. I'm used to it."

Fitz sat down in the front seat of his car and breathed deeply. It felt good to be alone with Buffett. "Hey, Bud. Sorry I've been gone so long. We have another one of those human problems going. You don't have to worry about stuff like this."

Buffett purred and nudged Fitz's chin.

"Thanks for the encouragement. I guess I'd better get going. I'll be back soon. Here's a prize." Fitz laid several treats on the seat, picked up his Beretta, and popped three M&Ms into his mouth before going to meet Ben in the garage.

"Do you think we'll find her?" Ben asked as he backed the car out.

"I think this is our best shot so far."

After about fifteen minutes, they were approaching the venue.

"There it is," Ben announced. "Sparkles Stables. You'd think she could have come up with a more creative name."

"It is free advertising, though," Fitz replied.

Ben slowed and turned into the entrance. "I don't see any cars."

"No lights, either."

It was 5:34pm when Ben parked and still a couple of hours till dark, but the clouds made it look later than it was. They got out of the car and looked around. Two brown and white horses and one black one fed on grass in the pasture. There were two identical barns and four outbuildings lined up in a row.

"I'm guessing one barn is for horses and one is for the events," Ben said.

"You mean the horses aren't invited?" Fitz teased.

"Neeeeigh," Ben said in his best horse voice. "Where should we start?"

"If I were going to hide someone here, I think I'd use one of the outbuildings."

"Or the venue barn. It might have lots of nooks and crannies."

"True," Fitz said. "But what if, like us, someone came to tour the place to see if they wanted to have their wedding here?"

"Are you asking me to marry you?" Ben quipped.

Fitz scrunched his eyebrows together. "No, I'm just saying I think it would be smarter to use an outbuilding. Let's get started." Fitz led the way to the closest one.

All of the buildings were painted the same barn red. The outbuildings were all the same, giving the property a planned, uniform appearance.

Fitz approached the first one and tested the door. It was locked, so he knocked. "Anyone here?" he called.

With no answer, they moved on to the second building and knocked again.

"Did you hear that?" Ben said.

"Hear what?"

"Shhh."

"Help! Help!" Came a call from the third building. It differed from the others in that it had a ramp leading up to the door

Fitz and Ben hurried over. "Victoria, is that you?"

"Help! Get me out of here!"

"Hold on and calm down," Fitz said. "We have to find a way to get the door open."

"Let me get the tire iron," Ben said.

"That's almost as good as a crowbar," Fitz said as Ben took off toward the car.

"Victoria, this is Fitz. We're going to get you out of there."

"Thank God you're here! I thought I was going to die."

Ben came hustling back with the tire iron and jack.

"Are you planning on jacking up the building?"

"No, I thought this would make a good hammer."

"If I had brought my car, I might have been able to pick the lock," Fitz said.

Ben set to pounding on the wood where the dead bolt entered the frame and shouted, "Hindsight is twenty-twenty."

With the noise he was making, they didn't hear the Hummer pull into the driveway. Fitz just happened to turn around and noticed the huge man getting out.

"We should have thought of security cameras before now, too."

"What?" Ben asked, continuing to pound.

Fitz touched him on the arm. "We have company."

As Ben turned to see what Fitz was talking about, the man reached behind him and pulled out a gun. "Don't move!" he shouted.

"That's our cue! Run to the back of the shed," Fitz urged.

They took off as fast as their old legs would let them. A shot boomed, and a bullet hit the shed just behind Fitz.

"He's not very friendly," Ben said as they leaned against the back of the shed.

They removed the safety from their weapons and cocked them. "Now what?" Ben asked.

"Get low and peek out to see where he's headed. But don't shoot. So far he doesn't know we're armed," Fitz directed, walking to the other corner.

They knelt and peeked around the corners of the building. Another shot hit the shed just above Fitz.

"I think he means to kill us first and ask questions later," Fitz whispered.

"I agree. It looks like he's headed toward the next shed, so he's playing it like we're armed," Ben whispered back.

Fitz looked out again and saw the man run behind the shed that was closest to the side he was on. "He's over here. Give me the tire iron, and you draw him this way." Fitz hustled to the other side of the shed behind which the man had run, tire iron in one hand and Beretta in the other.

He leaned into the side of the building, not sure what to do next. *OK, now what? He'll come around one side of the building, but I can't be at both corners.* He looked back and could still see Ben positioned at the far side of the shed he had just left. Clarity came, and he holstered the gun. *I'll give him five seconds before I move to the other corner.* Before he even started counting, he saw Ben rush around to the other side as a shot fired.

Fitz readied the tire iron and stood still. He could hear careful steps. The steps stopped just around the corner. He held his breath. Finally, a hand with a gun rounded the corner, then immediately pulled back. Fitz waited.

When the gun appeared the second time, Fitz swung down with all his might. The gun flew from the man's hand. Fitz rounded the corner and delivered a second blow to the man's head while he was still recoiling from the first blow. The man hit the ground and lay still as death.

Ben joined Fitz and said, "Nice job." He picked up the fallen gun. "I think he just saved us some trouble." He leaned down and unfastened a key ring from the man's belt.

"How much do you want to bet this was the guy who gave Katía the creeps the other day?" Fitz asked.

"He gives me the creeps even lying on the ground. That's one big dude."

Fitz checked for a pulse. "He's alive. We'd better get Victoria and get out of here."

They went back to the door and could hear crying from within. "It's OK, Victoria. We're going to get you out of here," Ben said as he searched through the keys. It took three tries before he got the right one.

"The monster is still down," Fitz noted, keeping an eye on the man.

Ben opened the door, and Victoria rushed in for a hug. "Thank you and thank God! I thought I would die in there."

Fitz hoped she wouldn't come to him next and said, "We have to go." He hurried toward the car.

"Do you think we could swap vehicles? His is nicer than mine," Ben quipped.

"Then you would have committed two crimes today," Fitz said.

"I don't consider rescuing Victoria a crime."

"The police would think otherwise since the Sparkles folks will fail to mention they had a hostage in the shed."

"You sure know how to spoil a guy's hopes."

"We'll worry about your crushed hopes later. Just get in the car and drive before reinforcements show up."

"Or before that mountain wakes up," Ben replied.

They hopped into the car, and Ben sped out of Clermont. After a few minutes of silence, Ben asked, "Fitz, why do you think that guy showed up when he did?"

"I'm sure they have security cameras on the property."

"Exactly."

"Are you thinking what I'm thinking?"

"Probably."

"We've got big problems."

CHAPTER 23

Fitz popped three M&Ms into his mouth. Time seemed to stand still as the scenery moved by while they drove south on Hwy. 129.

"How long do you think we have?" Ben asked.

"It depends on whether anyone else was monitoring the security cameras. If it was just that guy, then we have till he wakes up. If anyone else noticed, then they're probably already after us."

"We should have snatched that guy's phone," Ben replied.

"I wish you'd thought of that at the time."

"What are you talking about?" Victoria asked.

"The Sparkles owner will be trying to hunt us down. She can't afford for this to get out," Ben answered. "Do you have any idea why they abducted you?"

"She wanted me to steal drugs from the clients. I didn't want to and told her I wanted to quit after my shift yesterday. When I came to clock out, I went to the office to turn in my name tag, and this huge man grabbed me and brought me here. He told me I had till today to decide if I lived or died."

"Wow. So we were just in time," Ben said.

Fitz stewed over the situation, trying to come up with a plan. Then it hit him. "Katía and Luna will be in danger, too."

Ben's eyes scrunched. "You're right. I'm guessing they'll have Victoria's address on file, which puts her family in the line of danger, too."

"Do you think she will go after my husband and daughter?" Victoria asked, each word laced with dread.

"We need to let everyone know," Ben said.

"That's true, but first we need a plan," Fitz replied. "What are we going to do?"

*　*　*　*　*

Like cold molasses, consciousness oozed back to Victor Palfrey. He rolled his six-foot-four, two-hundred-eighty-pound self onto his back. His eyes slowly opened and saw the side of a building, trees, and a darkening sky.

My head hurts. He finally came to enough to touch the source of pain and pulled back bloody fingers. *Somebody hit me in the head.* Awareness started returning. He remembered where he was and what he had been doing.

After struggling to his feet, he checked the shed for the hostage he had come to kill. She was gone as he expected. A surge of rage roared into his body. It was mostly directed at himself. *How could I have been so careless? How could I have failed? They were just two old men!*

The next thought made him even angrier. *I have to let Crystal know.* He was surprised to find his phone in his pocket. *Idiots.* He wasn't surprised to find his keys were gone.

With his head aching and spinning, he walked to the Hummer while trying to compose what he would tell Crystal. *If I take a few extra minutes, it won't matter. She won't know when I regained consciousness. Oh, yeah. The security cameras.*

Still, he didn't rush to call. He checked the Hummer in the off chance that the keys might be there. They weren't. Leaning against the front seat, he pulled up Crystal's number. After hesitating a moment to go over what he would say, he placed the call.

"Hey, Victor. What's up?"

"When I came to get Victoria's final answer, there were two men trying to break her out. Somehow one of them got the jump on me and knocked me out. They took the woman."

"That's sloppy work, Victor. That's not what I pay you for. Now we have a real mess to contain."

Victor's face contorted with anger at the insult. He was glad this wasn't a video call. "I'm sorry, ma'am."

"Can you work or do you need to go to the hospital?"

"I believe I can work."

"Good. I need you here. Now." She disconnected before Victor could tell her that they took his keys.

He rubbed his head and set about trying to hotwire the Hummer, using his phone as a flashlight. The pain increased as he leaned down. *I forgot to ask where 'here' is. Will she be at the house or the office? My brain is a little off.*

His right hand was swollen. Stiffness and pain made working the wires harder. His vision became fuzzy. *I'd better sit up and be still a minute.* Sliding to the ground, he leaned against the Hummer and cradled his right hand.

When his vision cleared, he moved his right fingers, then the wrist. *Everything moves, so I don't guess it's broken.* Feeling more confident, he crawled back under the steering wheel and succeeded in starting the vehicle.

Do I go to the office or her house?

* * * * *

Crystal drummed her left fingers on the desk while she worked the mouse with her right hand to scan the security camera footage from the venue. When she saw the Outback pull into the parking area, she slowed down to watch two men get out.

She followed along as they walked to the outbuildings and discovered Victoria. One headed back to the car, and she zoomed in on the face. The low light made the image even grainier.

"That looks like one of the guys in the parking lot today," she said to herself. The doorbell startled her, and her chair rolled back from her jumping at the sound. She went to the door and let Shannon in.

"What are we going to do?" Shannon asked, wringing her hands as she walked into the house.

"We are going to find these people and silence them. We can't afford to be exposed. We have to stop it." Crystal eyed Shannon. "I need you to pull it together and help me come up with a plan." She led Shannon back to her home office.

Crystal and Shannon had been friends since high school. They both had married, then divorced with no children. When Crystal concocted her plan to use undocumented immigrants to steal a supply of opioids to sell, Shannon agreed to help. She fully believed the notion parroted by some politicians that all immigrants were rapists, murderers, or drug dealers, so she had no qualms with the trap Crystal set for her housecleaners … at least not until now.

"We have to find these people and eliminate them," Crystal said as she sat down at the computer. "Pull up the security footage from the office this afternoon when those people came to talk to the workers."

Shannon sat at the second desk and pulled up the footage, locating when the four pulled into the parking lot. "Got it," she said.

"I think the two guys at the office are the same two who nabbed the prisoner."

Shannon isolated the men, zoomed in, unplugged the laptop, and set it beside Crystal's. "The one with the long beard is definitely the same. It's harder to tell about the other one."

"He's the same, I guarantee it. Now we just have to identify them and track them down."

"What about the two women?" Shannon asked.

"They have to go, too. I suspect they're all in this together."

"Why were they be looking for that woman? How did they know she was at the venue?" Shannon wrung her hands again.

"I can see you're nervous, but we're going to handle it, OK? Victor should be here soon." She checked her watch. "Actually he should already be here. What's taking him so long," she growled. "Let's get back to identifying our perpetrators."

"I'm not sure I like the idea of killing white people," Shannon stated.

Crystal leveled her gaze on Shannon and tried to exude compassion. "Shannon, we don't have any other choice. They will ruin us if they get to the police. We'll both end up in prison. You don't want that, do you?"

"No, I don't want that."

"Good. Now help me find a way to identify these four people."

Crystal went back to studying the video footage from the venue. She saw Victor arrive, fire at the two men, then disappear behind an outbuilding. The next movement was the two men coming to unlock the door and lead Victoria to their vehicle. It backed out of the lot, so she never saw the tag.

"The only thing I have here is their faces and the car. I couldn't see the tag."

Shannon was writing on a note pad. "I have two tag numbers." She pulled off the note and handed it to Crystal. "I'm not sure that will help, though. I think the police and DMV are the only ones who can identify to whom the cars belong."

"True. We might have to enlist their help, then."

The doorbell rang. "It's about time he got here," Crystal fumed.

CHAPTER 24

Fitz tugged at his beard and ate more M&Ms as Ben drove south. *One thing I'm sure of. She'll do everything she can to keep her secret safe, which means eliminating us.* After thinking it through, he said, "I think we have to find a place to hide. As soon as she identifies us, we'll be in her crosshairs."

"What does that mean?" Victoria asked.

"She'll be out to kill us. That's the only way she can keep the truth from getting out."

"Do you think that man would really have killed me? He said he would if I didn't agree to steal pills for them."

"If you hadn't agreed to that demand, I'm sure of it," Fitz answered. "He was going to kill us just for trying to break you out."

"I hope you've come up with a plan. All I have is that we need to get out of our houses," Ben said.

"I don't have a house," Fitz replied.

"You know what I mean."

"Yeah. I'll start calling Katía and Luna. Head to your house so you can pack a bag and we can get the critters."

"That's all you've got?" Ben asked.

"I'm working on it!" Fitz answered.

Ben drove to his house while Fitz called Katía and Luna to tell them that they had to grab bags and get out of the house.

"What about my husband?" Luna asked.

"Bring him with you."

"Where are we going?"

"I don't know yet. Just get out as quickly as you can and bring supplies in case you have to sleep in the car. It would be better to leave in your husband's vehicle."

Next Fitz had Victoria call her husband and give him the news.

Victoria choked up. "Amor, it's me. I'm safe. The men rescued me." She went on to explain what was going on. "You and Sofía have to leave the house. She will be hunting me. Bring blankets so we can sleep in the car." She turned to Fitz. "Where do I tell him to meet us?"

"Think, think, think." Fitz tugged at his beard. "Let's meet at Little River Park. It's across the highway from your house."

As Ben pulled into the garage, Fitz sent a message on the group chat. "Let's meet at Little River Park in 30 minutes."

They got out of the car, and Ben offered, "You're welcome to wait in the house while I pack."

"I'm going to check on Buffett and head on to the park in case anyone's early," Fitz said. He took a deep breath and let it out slowly on his way to the car.

Sitting down in the driver's seat, he said to Buffett, "It's good to be home." Buffett greeted him with a rub to the chin.

"I missed you, too. We've gotten ourselves into a jam. I just hope we can survive it."

"Meow." Another rub to the chin.

"I see. Did you eat all the food?" Fitz checked the dish and found it empty. "Sorry. We'll have to remedy that immediately." Buffett started eating while he was still pouring the cat food.

"You'll have to eat while I drive. I need to get to the park."

The sound of crunching cat food was the only reply.

It was dark when Fitz pulled into a parking space at Little River Park. True to its name, the park was quite small, with just a few parking spaces and a boat ramp. Fitz was the only one there.

He laid the Beretta on the console and leaned his head back against the headrest to think. Buffett curled up in his lap, and Fitz stroked the cat's fur while pondering their situation. *We could call in the police, but that might cost Victoria and her family deportation. We also need to find Crystal's stash of pills as evidence. Right now she could just deny knowledge of the situation and pin it on the goon. Most importantly, we have to stay alive. We need a place to hide. I wonder if she has more goons than the one I hit over the head. I hope that guy's not dead even though he was trying to kill us. I guess I should have called an ambulance.*

Approaching lights drew Fitz's attention away from his thoughts. He gripped the gun while waiting to see who it was. He felt like a sitting duck. Finally the lights turned, and Luna and her husband parked next to him.

He got out and greeted them.

"Why do you think we need to leave our home and go hide?" Carlos asked.

"The woman who is after us knows our tag numbers and has images of our faces. She is well connected in the county and could call in some favors to help identify us. Since she already tried to kill Ben and me, I don't think she will hesitate to send hit men after all of us. If her secret gets out, she's ruined."

"I'm afraid that makes sense," Carlos said.

"I brought lasagna for everyone," Luna chimed in.

"How did you have time to make lasagna?" Fitz marveled.

"I was cooking it for Carlos and me anyway. I always make a big pan and freeze it."

Two more cars rolled into the park. It was Ben followed by Sofía and Alejandro, Victoria's husband.

Sofía jumped out and grabbed Victoria in a bear hug. Then she ran to Fitz and hugged him. "Thank you so much for saving Mamá!"

Fitz's spine stiffened, but he slowly relaxed and hugged her back. Ben gladly received her hug next.

Two more sets of lights coming caused Fitz's spine to stiffen again. He pulled the gun out. "One of those is probably Katía, but who's the other one?"

As they got closer, Ben said, "It sounds like Zee."

Zee groaned a bit getting out of the car. "Why we meetin' here this time of night?"

"A lot has happened since this morning," Ben said, then went on to explain what had led to meeting at the park.

"That's some pickle," Zee agreed. "I'm happy to help if I can. Are we stayin' here tonight?"

Fitz could only imagine the faces of the typically housed folks after Zee's question. "I think we need a place with more facilities."

"I think we'll go to a hotel," Carlos said.

"That's not a good idea," Fitz answered. "If she has connections with law enforcement, she could locate where credit cards were used. If you have cash, I guess that would work."

"We need a place with beds, a bathroom, and a kitchen that she doesn't know about. I wonder if the building that the evil doctor was using is still set up," Ben said.

Fitz tugged at his beard and ate more M&Ms. *It's tempting. Suddenly having six cars in the parking lot would be a red flag. Plus we'd have to break in.* After his ponderings, he said, "I think it's risky. We don't even know who owns the building now. I think our best bet for tonight is Walmart. We can back in at the edge of the lot so our tags aren't obvious."

"I'm for whatever keeps Mamá safe," Sofía said.

"I suppose there is a reason we don't just call the police and have her arrested," Luna wondered.

Fitz answered, "I can think of three. One, calling the police means Victoria would have to tell what happened, which would risk her family's deportation. Two, all we have so far is that the goon locked her in the shed at the venue. Samson could throw him under the bus and walk away free. Third, we have no stash of pills to verify Victoria's story."

"I was afraid you'd have a good reason. At least we have lasagna. I hope everyone's hungry," Luna replied.

"Yum. That sounds delicious," Zee said.

"There's light at Walmart. Why don't we drive there first? Everyone back into a space on the garden center side," Fitz directed.

"Oh man, that's where I just came from. I could have saved the gas," Zee griped.

CHAPTER 25

Crystal studied Ben's and Fitz's faces till they were burned into her memory. Then she studied the two women. "All four of these are liabilities. I'm sure they're working together. Victor, I hope you brought lots of ammo."

Victor, sitting across the room with an icepack on his head said, "I have plenty."

"So far, we have two tag numbers and four people to identify. We know where that woman lives. Maybe she should be our first target. They've had time to get her home. Victor, go to the woman's house, what was her name?"

"Victoria, ma'am," Shannon said.

"Get to the house and deal with anyone who is there. Find out if the whole family is present first, though," Crystal directed.

"Yes, ma'am." Victor groaned as he got up from the chair.

"Are you sure you're up to this?"

"I'll handle it."

"I don't care what the body count is, I want this contained ASAP."

With Victor gone, Shannon said, "The images aren't great, but I'm going to run them through a facial recognition program to see if we get any hits. This Black woman is the clearest. I'll start with her."

Crystal paced. Fear that her empire was crumbling coursed through her veins. *I've managed so far. I will conquer this, too. I just have to be methodical and tie up the loose ends. Identify and eliminate is the plan. Step by step. One by one. What's the next step? Oops.*

"Shannon, call Victor and tell him not to engage if the police are on the scene."

"I don't think they'd call the police since they're illegal, but I'll call him."

Crystal checked her watch. "It should take Victor about half an hour to finish up there. We need the next target by then."

"The program is running," Shannon said after disconnecting from Victor. "I can run another one on your computer to speed things up."

"Why didn't I think of that? Get it going."

Shannon's computer pinged while she was loading Ben's image into the facial recognition program on Crystal's computer.

Crystal hurried over. "I hope they're all this easy!" Hope mixed with her angst as she read the screen. "Katía Bancroft.

She's a pastor. What a pity. She shouldn't have gotten mixed up in this."

She whipped out her phone and did a search for "Katía Bancroft Gainesville, GA." Scanning the results, she remarked, "Well, look at that. She's quite forthcoming. We have her address and the fact that she's single."

Crystal opened the text app on her phone but decided texting Victor would be a mistake. She called instead. "When you're done there, I have the next address for you. Call me. No texts. And remember, we can't leave any witnesses." She disconnected and resumed pacing.

Shannon entered Fitz's image for recognition and set it to searching. "If I were them, I would have already called the police."

Crystal stopped in her tracks and seared Shannon with her gaze. "We aren't in handcuffs, are we? We can't think negatively. We have to keep pressing forward. I will contain this situation. … I have to."

Crystal's phone rang with the ringtone that identified Victor's call. "How did it go?" she asked.

"No one's here. The house is empty."

After releasing a stream of vulgarities, she gave him Katía's address. "Get over there quickly. I should have the next target's address by the time you're done there."

Crystal leaned against the wall. "It's going to be a long night."

CHAPTER 26

Luna dished up the lasagna from the back of Carlos's CR-V. "This is just like tailgating for a football game," she said.

"I ain't eaten this good in a long time," Zee said. "You're a fine cook!"

They fished water and sodas from a cooler that Luna had brought. While the rest of the crew leaned on cars and chatted as they ate, Fitz and Ben withdrew to the other side of Fitz's Highlander.

"When this is all over, maybe we can convince the prosecutor to give Victoria a deal and not pursue deportation in exchange for her testimony," Ben said.

"That's a good idea, but we still need more evidence to catch Samson. So far the goon is the only one we can incriminate," Fitz said.

"The goon and ourselves, that is. Victoria can testify that she was forced to steal pills," Ben replied.

"It's just her word against Samson's. I'm betting the jury would believe Samson."

"You're probably right. What if we could convince some of the other workers to testify?"

"That would help, but we still don't have any hard evidence. We can't get to the workers, either. We need the pills… Or we need to catch her in the act of distributing them," Fitz said.

"That's probably the goon's job, too," Ben said. "Do you think she keeps the pills at the venue?"

"I wondered that, too. It makes sense. They could be in one of the outbuildings."

"We should have searched while we were there."

"Now you think of that. I guess we could always go back," Fitz mused.

"If you're thinking what I think you're thinking, it's going to be a long night," Ben said. "And we don't have any coffee."

"Who says we don't have coffee?" Fitz asked. "I can make some in a hurry."

"What are you two yakking about?" Fitz jumped at Katía's sudden presence.

"Fitz was just telling me he can be our barista if we want coffee," Ben answered.

"Umm hmm. I'm guessing you were planning something. If not, that's what we need to be doing. No offense, Fitz, but I don't relish the idea of living in my car for the next month or two."

Fitz looked at the ground, not wanting to share what they had been discussing. An awkward pause ensued.

"Look, guys. You're not that hard to read. Go ahead and spill the beans," Katía said.

"We were talking about going back to the venue and looking for her stash of stolen pills," Ben caved.

Fitz shot him a look, but Ben continued. "Fitz says that if we don't have direct evidence to tie the Sparkles owner to the crime, then she can claim it was all done by the goon that shot at us."

"Is there any point in waiting? Let's go," Katía replied. "And before you say it, I know it could be dangerous. These people need to be stopped before they ruin other lives."

"OK. But it's just the three of us," Fitz said. "I'm not risking any more lives. Plus having this whole crew there would create a wider target."

"I guess the coffee will have to wait," Ben groaned.

Everyone was finishing up their meals when Luna said, "I have brownies and coffee if you want dessert."

Ben grinned. "I'm all in.

As they enjoyed the dessert, Fitz explained what Ben, Katía, and he were going to do. He ended with, "Do any of the rest of you have a gun?"

They shook their heads.

"Do any of you know how to use a gun?"

Alejandro answered, "In the neighborhood we left behind, being armed and ready was a necessity. Victoria and I are both competent with firearms."

"I'm glad to hear that," Fitz said as he opened the liftgate of his Highlander. He fished out two Berettas and loaded them. Handing them over to Alejandro, he said, "I hope you don't need these. Remember the store closes at eleven, so tend to any needs before then.

"I'll be glad to drive," Katía said.

Ben, Fitz, and Katía started for her car, then Fitz said, "Wait. Let's go in Ben's car. They haven't seen yours yet, and that might come in handy later."

Ben drove past the venue and parked on the side of the road. They came up through the woods behind the four outbuildings.

As they approached, Fitz whispered, "As soon as we step out from behind the buildings, they'll be able to see us. We'll have to move fast. You have the key ready?"

"I hope so. I think this is the one."

"Remember, unlock all of them so if one of us finishes our building we can start on the remaining one. Let's go. I want us out of here before they have a chance to respond."

"You know this is illegal, right?" Ben said.

"So is forcing women to steal opioids," Katía said.

"Just checking," Ben replied.

They hurried to the building in which Victoria had been locked. Fitz tried the door, and it opened. "It looks like the goon forgot to lock it up."

"We did have his key," Ben said.

"Oh, yeah. I've got this one. Y'all get started on the next one."

While Ben and Katía hurried to the next buildings, Fitz turned on his phone's flashlight. There wasn't much in there, just a couple of saddles, a huge mower, a couple of blowers and weed trimmers, and fuel containers. After a quick scan of the rafters and floor, he moved to the fourth building. He could hear shuffling as he passed the other two.

What if we don't find anything? We will have exposed ourselves for nothing. She could have us arrested… if they can find us. He popped three M&Ms into his mouth.

He opened the door to the last building to find it filled with plastic bins. Scanning the boxes, he saw they were labeled with descriptions of holiday decorations. *Oh, boy. This is going to be a nightmare.*

Cross-shaped aisles offered access to the mountains of bins. He tugged his beard and decided to start at the back and work his way to the front. *Katía and Ben should be here soon. She could have pills in any of these boxes.*

Taking the left branch of the cross, he started at the end. Written with Sharpies on the side and tops of the bins was the name of the holiday. *It starts with New Year, Winter, Valentine's Day. They're in order.*

He stood, puzzling. There were hundreds of bins. *We don't have time to go through all of these, which makes this the perfect place to hide a stash of narcotics.*

The bins labeled Easter/Spring were empty. *On the other hand, if she has staff who decorate, she wouldn't risk their discovering the stash mixed in with the decorations ... unless she comes in and moves them so they're in with a holiday that is not coming up.*

Deciding that St. Patrick's Day was too close to the current bins, he backed up one more and began pulling out the Valentine's Day bins. He stacked them in the aisle without looking, expecting any pills to be hidden at the bottom in the very back.

Fitz jumped, nearly dropping a bin, when Katía stepped in and said, "Whoa! What is this?"

"It's their supply of decorations," Fitz answered, recovering his composure.

"I guess it would take a lot to decorate that barn. You're not planning to go through all of these, are you?"

"No. I'm guessing that if they're here, they'd be mixed in with recent holiday bins. Why don't you tackle New Year/Winter?"

"Umm."

Fitz looked and realized he was taking all the aisle space with the bins he was moving. "Oh. Well check through those to be sure there are no pills."

As Katía stepped into the aisle, a small red dot on the wall caught Fitz's attention. Clambering over the bins, he whispered, "Get down!"

"What is it?"

"A laser sight just hit the wall. I think our goon is here already." Then he called out to Ben, "We have company, and he has a laser sight."

As Fitz finished his sentence a shot rang out. A second and a third shot sounded.

"You OK, Ben?" Fitz called.

"Yeah, and I'm hoping his Hummer is dead in the water. I think he has a rifle, so be careful," Ben called back.

"We're stuck in the building."

Fitz heard running footsteps that stopped behind their building. Then Ben's low voice came through. "I'll keep him occupied while you two get out of there."

"OK." Fitz then whispered to Katía, "You ready?"

"As ready as I'll ever be."

"When we go out, run to the side opposite of where Ben is firing."

"Got it."

Fitz steeled his muscles, hoping they would move fast enough to get him to safety.

CHAPTER 27

Crystal plopped down into a chair in her home office, the initial adrenaline surge starting to fade and leaving her fatigued. "This will be three down. That leaves what… five or six to go?"

"It depends on whether or not any of them have children," Shannon answered. "I can't believe they were dumb enough to go back to the venue."

Crystal slammed her hand onto the arm of the chair. "That woman must have told them about the pills."

"Why wouldn't she?" Shannon asked, her voice sounding testy.

A ping on Shannon's computer signaled another match by the facial recognition program. Crystal hurried over.

"We have names for all four of them," Shannon said as she looked over Luna's photo from social media.

"I'll check out her social media, you look for her address," Crystal directed. It took her less than thirty seconds to discover that Luna was married with two grown children. "She has a husband," she commented flatly.

"Not that it's going to matter since they're on the run, but I have her address," Shannon announced.

"Good job." Crystal's attention drifted back to her computer screen where the video footage of the venue was pulled up. She could see Victor's hummer. Three flashes of light came from the outbuildings followed by two from near the Hummer.

"Of course they're armed," she muttered.

"While Victor deals with those three, we need to get back to figuring out how to locate the others," Shannon said.

Crystal's glare would have shriveled most people, but Shannon had known her since high school. Crystal could tell Shannon wasn't fazed.

"You're right. What's our next step?"

* * * * *

Fitz and Katía hovered at the corner of the two aisles, waiting for Ben to begin firing. Fitz saw the red dot return to the back wall of the outbuilding.

"He's aiming at chest height, so stay low," he whispered to Katía.

The sound of Ben's gun firing propelled Fitz into action. Scurrying out the building, he cut left, away from Ben, turned around the side of the building and ran behind it. Katía ran into him when he stopped.

"Sorry about that," she whispered.

Ben surged around the corner, pointed to the woods, and said, "Let's go. Try to keep on a straight line so the shed stays between us and him."

Katía took off and whispered, "Y'all try to keep up."

They bolted into the woods, thankful for the gibbous moon that helped them see at least a little. Fitz brought up the rear, holding his arms up, elbows bent ninety degrees, to fend off branches and briars.

After they had crashed through the woods about a hundred yards, Fitz whispered for them to stop. He listened for sounds of the goon following. The woods returned an eerie silence, except for the hoot of an owl in the distance.

Fitz pointed toward the road and took the lead, moving purposefully but as quietly as he could. It took almost ten minutes before the silver ribbon of the road shone in the moonlight ahead.

Fitz stopped about twenty feet from the tree line and scanned the road. Ben's car was two hundred feet to the left. "He'll know we're heading for the road, so he's probably out there somewhere," he whispered.

"Unless I hit him," Ben whispered back.

"Highly unlikely at that distance in the dark," Fitz answered.

"Hey, a guy could get lucky," Ben returned.

"I hope he doesn't have night vision on his scope," Katía said.

"If I were him, I'd wait somewhere in the woods near the car," Fitz whispered.

"We'll have to take our chances and hope we get lucky," Ben suggested.

The woods lit up ahead, signaling a vehicle approaching.

"It looks like he was too lazy to walk," Ben said. "I had hoped I disabled his Hummer."

"Get down," Fitz ordered.

They crouched in the woods and watched as the lights rounded the curve.

"That's not a Hummer," Ben whispered.

The vehicle slowed, and blue lights began to flash.

"This is our chance. Let's go," Ben said.

"Tuck away the guns," Fitz said as they hustled out of the woods, down the small bank, and back toward the car where the deputy was shining a flashlight inside.

"Hey, officer," Ben called.

The deputy shined his flashlight on Ben while moving behind the car.

"Hands up, please," the deputy called.

The three park pals complied and continued toward the car. Fitz was anxious to get inside and get out of there. *Will this guy kill an officer?*

"Do you mind telling me why you're parked on the side of the road and wandering around in the dark?"

Ben responded quickly. "A deer crossed ahead of us and it was limping badly. We thought we could help."

Fitz hoped the deputy didn't notice his surprise. The deputy paused, seeming to consider Ben's explanation.

"That's not very bright. Your car could have caused an accident, and judging by the sticks in your hair, you've been trespassing. Now get in the car and move on."

"Yes, sir," Ben said, and the trio wasted no time in doing just as the officer directed.

Fitz directed Ben back to Hwy. 129 without having to turn around and further raising the deputy's suspicions or passing by the shooter.

Katía breathed a sigh. "That was too close for comfort."

"I'm surprised the goon didn't fire on all four of us," Fitz said.

"Unless he was down back at the Hummer," Ben added.

"I think two lucky events in one night are too much to hope for," Fitz responded.

They continued on toward Gainesville, not noticing the Hummer that turned off a side road behind them.

CHAPTER 28

Fitz noticed Ben looking concerned. He kept checking the rearview mirror. "You look worried."

"I believe we're being followed by a Hummer," Ben answered as they approached the Little River bridge. "Get ready for a sudden turn."

A tenth of a mile past the bridge, Ben whipped to the left, hit the brakes, and screeched onto Lakeview Street. The Hummer's tires squealed as it sailed past the turn.

"I was right," Ben said, flooring the gas pedal and flying up the hill.

"You do know there's a stop sign up ahead," Fitz said.

"I'm going to consider that more of a suggestion tonight."

Fitz had a death grip on the armrest. "I think we should go back north when you get to Clarks Bridge. He'll be expecting us to go toward Gainesville."

"Great minds think alike," Ben replied.

Katía was keeping a watch out the back. "I see lights coming," she said as Ben careened onto Lakewood.

He hit the gas, driving as fast as he dared. When he got to the intersection with Clarks Bridge Road, he slowed, then took a quick left. He cut off his lights and drove by the moonlight.

Ten seconds later, Katía announced, "There he is."

The Hummer turned right, heading toward Gainesville.

"Way to go, Ben. You lost him," Katía said.

"Now where do we go?" Ben asked as he slowed back to the speed limit.

"He'll figure out that we went north soon. Will he turn around and chase us or go on toward Gainesville and lie in wait?" Fitz popped M&Ms into his mouth and thought.

"If I were him, I'd park at the old Riverbend Elementary School so I could catch us whether we came into town on Clarks Bridge or Cleveland Highway," Katía offered.

"You're right. That would be his best move. Do you think he's smart enough to figure that out?" Ben asked.

"The more likely thing to do is turn around and chase us up this road. Let's take Wiley Road and cut back over to Cleveland Highway. Then we can take Limestone over to Jesse Jewell and go back to Walmart that way," Fitz directed.

"Sounds like a plan to me," Ben said.

They made it back to Walmart without seeing the Hummer again and without having located a stash of pills. It was nearly one in the morning. The others greeted them as they got out of the car, except for Sofía, who was asleep in the back seat of Alejandro's gray Altima.

Snickers leaned into Ben, wagging her tail and licking with excitement. "Thanks for watching her, Zee," Ben said.

"No problem. She and King enjoyed visitin'."

"Well?" Luna asked, hands going to her hips.

"We didn't find anything. The goon showed up before we finished searching," Katía explained.

"That guy's getting on my nerves," Luna replied. "I found out that Sparkles employs twenty-five cleaners, and they serve over four hundred clients. That's a lot of opportunity to steal pills."

"I thought we agreed to leave our phones off," Fitz scolded.

"I didn't turn it on," Luna replied, hands back to her hips. "Walmart was kind enough to lend me a computer."

"I see. That was nice of them," Ben said.

"At least we're safe for now," Luna said, "But we need to come up with a plan to tie all of this to Crystal Samson. Remember my telling you about my aunt taking too many of her pills, Katía? Guess who cleans her house. Sparkles. I bet they've been stealing from her, too."

Ben yawned. "If I'm going to keep going, I'll need some of that coffee you promised."

"I'll get on that right now," Fitz said, thankful to have something to do. He thought better when he was busy at routine tasks. He set a pot of water to boil on the PocketRocket camp stove and located the jar of instant coffee. Leaning against the car, he let his mind wander. *Will she take time to move her stash or concentrate on hunting us down?... That's a hard one to call. I'd have to bet on her coming after us. She can still claim it's all on the goon at this point, even if authorities locate a stash of opioids on her property. We can certainly verify that it was the goon who came after us.*

"That's a nice gadget," Ben said. Fitz jumped, hands flying up.

"Thanks. It boils water in a hurry," he replied.

"What does it use for fuel?"

"It's a mix of isobutane and propane. I'm surprised how long one of the little canisters lasts." The pot emitted the hiss of water heating up.

"I have cups, if you need them," Katía called.

Relief washed over Fitz. "That would be helpful. I have two, but they only get rinsed out. People might prefer something more pristine."

Fitz asked for everyone's preference as to strength, then poured up four cups. He set another pot to boil for the rest of them.

"Oh, I almost forgot. Our goon has a name. Victor Palfrey. I found him listed as the property manager way down in the website," Luna announced.

"I wonder what this Victor's next move will be," Fitz said.

"Maybe he'll go home and go to bed," Ben quipped.

"Yeah, right," Katía said. "How are we going to catch these people without getting ourselves killed?"

"What do you mean, 'Without getting ourselves killed?'" Luna asked. "Is there something you're not telling me?"

"There was shooting involved at the venue," Ben answered.

"Oh, boy," Luna replied.

"We could go back to the venue and keep searching," Katía offered. "We'd have a while before Victor could get there."

"True, but she might expect that and have Victor lying in wait for us. What else could he do?" Fitz wondered.

"Ride around looking for our cars?" Ben suggested.

CHAPTER 29

Crystal slammed her fist onto the desk, making the laptop hop. Stuffing her phone back into her pocket, she said, "He lost them. How could he lose them? I think Victor's losing his edge."

"He has been hitting the opioids hard lately," Shannon said.

Crystal glared at her. Victor had free access to the pills the cleaners brought in for his personal use. It was one of the perks for what he did for Crystal. She hadn't expected him to go overboard.

"I'll have to have a chat with him once we get through this crisis."

"There it is. We have all of their cell numbers now," Shannon announced after having discovered Luna's.

"Great. Let's see if we can find them."

"How do you want me to pay?" Shannon asked.

Crystal thought a minute. *Shannon is smart. She knew better than to use a card that could be traced back to me.* She pulled out a prepaid Visa card and instructed Shannon to use it. She looked over Shannon's shoulders as she entered the first number into the shady program.

The timer spun for several seconds before returning, "No Response."

Expletives flowed before Crystal said, "Don't tell me they turned off their phones. Keep trying anyway."

Crystal resumed pacing and talking to herself. "Where could they hide? Probably a hotel. An Airbnb? We could send Victor around to those while we call hotels."

She pulled up the Airbnb app on her phone. "Wow. There are over seven hundred in the Gainesville area. That's ridiculous."

Crystal heard Shannon speaking. "Yes, we're having a family emergency, and I'm trying to locate Luna Castillo. Is this the hotel she checked into?... OK. Thanks."

While Shannon dialed the next hotel, Crystal tried to figure out what Victor could do to help.

It was 3:47am when Crystal's phone rang, nearly sending her through the roof. Checking the caller ID, she noted it was Joe Fitzgerald calling. "Quick, locate this number while his phone is on," she instructed Shannon.

Answering the call, she placed the phone on speaker and set it beside Shannon so she could read the number. "Hello."

"Hi, Crystal."

"Hey, Joe."

"Most people call me Fitz. We both know what time it is."

"And what time is that?"

"It's time for you to call off your hit man and turn yourself in."

"I have no idea what you're talking about, Fitz was it?"

"We met him at your venue."

"Oh, you must be the one who broke into my property and whom the police are looking for right now. I'd say it's time to turn yourself in."

"We both know you didn't call the police. It would be too risky."

Crystal stemmed the tidal wave of rage that flooded, trying to maintain control of her voice. "All I know is that I was a victim of a break-in, and I'm glad Victor was able to run you off before you and your crew stole anything. Using facial recognition, we were able to identify you, and the search is on to bring you to justice. Don't think you can mess with me and get away with it."

"You're right. What we did was wrong. I'll go ahead and turn myself in to the police and explain why we broke in and what we were looking for. I'll make sure they know about Victoria's abduction, too."

Crystal clenched her jaw so hard it hurt. "Again, I don't know what you're talking about. You seem to have a vivid imagination. Are you a druggie?"

"Ouch. That hurt. Hurt me to the quick."

Shannon pointed to the computer screen and nodded her head. Crystal noticed the blinking dot. Muting the phone, she said, "Get Victor out there."

She unmuted and said, "Mister, I don't know why you're harassing me, but I'm a forgiving soul and would be happy to talk with you about whatever is going on. Why don't we meet over coffee? Maybe I can help you resolve your issues."

Laughter erupted from the phone. Crystal couldn't help grinning. "OK, maybe you're not a people person. We could chat on the phone. Tell me about your troubles."

"That would be nice," sniffle. "As a child I was traumatized by an evil stepmother."

"Go on," Crystal grinned to Shannon.

"She was into stealing opioids from clients of her housecleaning service and selling them for profit. It was devastating to my develop…"

Crystal cut him off. "I'm not playing this game anymore." She was so angry that she disconnected the call, forgetting she needed to keep him talking as long as possible.

"Don't give me that look," Crystal said of Shannon's grimace. "I couldn't stand talking to him anymore."

"Victor's on his way and should be there in about ten minutes. I just hope they don't leave."

Crystal clenched her fists, as if that would cause Victor to move faster.

* * * * *

Victor had just swallowed two more oxycodone tablets for his aching head. He had lost track of how many he had taken. When Shannon texted the coordinates of Fitz's location, he was finishing up a serving of pancakes at Waffle House. "On my way," he texted back.

CHAPTER 30

Victor left a twenty dollar bill on the table for his meal and tip and hurried out the door. He entered the GPS coordinates into his phone and studied the location. Zooming in, he saw that the dot blinked beside a building. *They're on Martin Luther King, Junior Boulevard. At least I don't have to drive far.*

The pain in his head started to lessen, and the old familiar buzz from the oxycodone worked its magic as he cranked the Hummer and headed for his quarry. Because of his size, he believed he needed extra pain pills, but truth be told, he enjoyed the buzz they gave him. It wasn't enough to disable him but just enough to smooth life's rough edges.

He turned off E. E. Butler Parkway onto Martin Luther King and parked on the side of the road about a quarter mile from the blinking dot. *I believe this is a job for the Glock.* He placed three extra clips into his pocket and locked the Hummer as he left. With the Glock in one hand and the phone in the other, he made his way down the sidewalk toward the dot.

He moved behind a tree once he was within sight of the building beside which the blue dot blinked. *No cars? I wonder where they stashed them. Maybe behind the building?*

Victor didn't like surprises. He had expected to see the quarry's cars lined up in the parking lot. He scrunched his eyes, trying to think this through, the narcotics fuzzing his brain. *I guess it makes sense not to leave them out in the open where they're easier to find. I think I'll circle the building before I approach.*

Victor had had some army training in his early years. He had enlisted at eighteen, discovered he didn't like the rigors of army life, and got out as soon as he could. Now at forty-one, he tried to recall some of the things they had drilled into him.

The memory *I need to know as much about the situation I'm entering as I can* worked its way through the fog. He went back to the last intersection and followed the sidewalk, taking the full block around the building. From the street behind the building, he could see no cars there, either.

They must have parked somewhere else. That was smart. I'd better not underestimate these folks.

Working out a path in his mind, he set off, crossed a parking lot behind the building, and hurried to the backside. There was a loading bay door but no windows. He tested the door. It was locked. *What will I do if the front door is locked? Ugh, I'm not thinking clearly. I shouldn't have taken the pain pills. At least my head feels better. There's only one way to find out.*

He moved to the corner, peeked around and quickly pulled his head back. Having seen no one, he looked around again. With the coast clear, he moved toward the front corner.

He paused and listened. Hearing no one, he peeked around the corner and saw nothing but a bucket sitting by the door. It was turned upside down. *If the door is locked, I'll have to shoot the lock out and then enter in a hurry. Or would it be better to wait until they come out? Oh, well, I'll figure it out as I go.*

Looking again, he noticed the security camera on the far corner. It was aimed at the parking lot, so he believed he could stay close to the building and not be seen.

When he reached the front door, he checked his phone again. It showed he was right on top of Fitz's phone. Scrunching his eyes, he wondered what that meant. *Are they just on the other side of the door? What is that bucket doing here?*

Out of curiosity, he bent down and turned the bucket over to find a cell phone lying on the ground. Bending down to pick it up, he heard, "Freeze and drop the gun!"

The sound startled him so that he fell forward. A knee landed between his shoulder blades, and he felt the barrel of a gun on his temple.

"Let go of the gun. If you move, you're a dead man."

Victor opened his hand and moved it away from the gun. Someone snatched it then the knee moved.

"Hands behind your back. Zip ties, please, and shoot him if he moves."

"I think he's stoned," a woman's voice said.

"Get up, if you can," the original man's voice said.

Victor struggled to his feet and found three guns pointed at his heart. Fitz picked up his phone and turned it off. "Oops, they lost us. What is Crystal going to say about this?" Fitz chided.

"Fitz? I was supposed to kill you, but you caught me. How could that happen?" Victor said. The pain medication, now in full force, was clouding his mind more than he realized.

"Your being stoned made it a lot easier than we expected," Katía said.

The other man took his phone, then frisked him, taking his extra clips and knife.

Fitz grabbed his arm and pulled. "Let's go. Make sure to turn off his phone."

They deposited Victor into Ben's Outback and drove off.

"Thanks for cooperating," Fitz said, seated beside him with his gun trained at his heart.

Victor didn't respond, his thoughts bouncing randomly. *How am I going to get out of this? What is Crystal going to say? I shouldn't have gotten caught. Are they going to kill me? What am I going to do? Who'll feed my cat?*

CHAPTER 31

Ben parked beside the others' cars at Walmart, and Luna, Carlos, Victoria, and Alejandro congratulated them as they got out.

"The plan worked like a charm," Katía said. "He looks like he's high on something, which helped.

"That's one threat neutralized. I wonder if she has any other hit men on her payroll," Ben said.

"We need to have someone keep an eye on this guy," Fitz said.

"I'll take the first shift if you'll make another round of coffee," Katía replied. She leaned against Fitz's car, which was parked next to Ben's, and waved her pistol at Victor so he would know she was armed. His eyes didn't seem to focus.

"He's not looking so good," she called to Fitz and Ben, who were preparing coffee.

"I bet he's been sampling his boss's merchandise," Ben replied.

Katía walked to the front of the car to check on the coffee's progress. When she returned, Victor had fallen over sideways, lying half on and half off the seat.

"Guys, he fell over. This looks bad," she said.

"Mind the stove, and I'll go check," Fitz said. He looked through the back window at the huge man, who looked dead. "This could be a ploy to escape. I'm going to the other side. We'll open the doors at the same time, then I'll lean in and check for a pulse. If he grabs me, shoot him in the leg. Keep shooting till he lets go."

"Got it," Katía replied.

Fitz nodded and together they pulled the back doors open. After a pause, Fitz leaned in and whacked Victor on the shoulder three times. "Hey, wake up!" After getting no response, he felt for the carotid pulse. "He's still alive. I'm guessing he either took too much pain medicine or it's the head injury from my whacking him. Either way, he needs medical attention."

"We can get Zee to call an ambulance," Katía suggested. By then the whole gang had gathered at the front of the car.

"If we call for an ambulance the police and fire department will come, too," Fitz said. "We'd be exposed. I think it'll be better if we take him to the emergency room. We can get him there about as quickly as an ambulance could get here."

"Man, I was looking forward to some coffee," Ben said.

"It'll have to wait. I don't want this guy to be dead when we get there," Fitz replied. "Katía, can you manage the stove? Just cut it off when everyone's had enough coffee."

"Sure. I have one of these at home. Good luck on the delivery."

Ben and Fitz hopped into the car and took off. "Do you think we should let Crystal know her goon is going to the ER?" Ben wondered.

"Hmm," Fitz pondered. He could see potential dangers either way. "If we let her know, then she can immediately begin looking for other ways to take us out. If we don't give the ER folks her contact information, they're going to want ours."

"Now that's a conundrum," Ben replied. "What are we going to tell them when we drop him off?"

"I think we should say we found him in… we need a parking lot other than Walmart's. Is there anything open this time of night?"

"Waffle House is the only thing I can think of."

"Perfect," Fitz said. "We found him in the parking lot there and brought him in."

"Why didn't we call an ambulance?" Ben asked, playing devil's advocate.

"Because we thought we could get him to the ER quicker than an ambulance could."

"And since we know nothing about him, there's no need to provide contact information."

"We should have checked his wallet," Ben said. "He might have Crystal's card or something."

"Still, I wonder if there are any advantages to letting her know he's out of commission. It might prompt her to give up."

A snort erupted from Ben. "You don't seriously believe a woman like that would just give up and turn herself in, do you?"

"Yeah, I guess that's wishful thinking. If we stop at a redlight, I'm going to get in the back and go through his wallet."

"Be careful," Ben said. "He might wake up."

The traffic light at Jesse Jewell and John Morrow brought them to a stop. Fitz hopped out and got into the back. "That felt like when we played Chinese Fire Drill as teenagers," Fitz chuckled.

"Yeah, but you could make it all the way around the car back then."

"Oh shut up and drive."

As Ben proceeded, Fitz fished the wallet out of Victor's back pocket. Using the cabin light, he scanned the contents. "Nothing incriminating here. No pictures of family, either."

"I don't think many people keep pictures in their wallets anymore. They're all on cell phones. Speaking of that, should we give them his cell phone?"

Fitz didn't reply. He did keep a photo in his wallet. It was the most precious thing he owned: a picture of Sharon. Ben's comment sent him into that dark place her loss had left in his soul, triggering the memory of when he had received the terrible call.

One of her platoon mates, who knew of their relationship, had called to tell him she was dead. He thought he had literally heard his heart break when he heard those words. It was a dark time, and it still seemed just as fresh and painful as it had in that moment. *If only I had been able to say goodbye, to hold her one more time, to ease the pain she must have felt.*

The scenery passing by didn't register as he wiped at tears rolling down his cheeks.

"Hey. You still back there?" Ben's words brought Fitz back to the present.

I'm in a car with Ben going to the hospital. "Yeah, I'm still back here."

"You didn't hear me ask about his phone, did you?"

"No, I guess I missed that."

"Should we put it back in his pocket?"

"Right now, I don't care what we do."

"What's going on? Something's wrong," Ben said.

"Sorry. I just went somewhere that's hard to be. Let me get back with it. The phone… If we give it back, Crystal will be able to locate him. If we don't, … I can't think of any negative consequences. Let's dump it at the Waffle House parking lot where we found him."

"That's a stroke of genius!" Ben replied as he slowed to turn into the hospital campus. He parked in front of the emergency room entrance. "Our story is that we stopped in to have a bite at Waffle House and found this guy lying…"

"How about at the tree line just off the asphalt?" Fitz suggested.

"Perfect. And that's all we know about him. Did we pick him up, or was he able to help us get him into the car?"

"Let's say at that time he could help. I wouldn't want to pick this guy up," Fitz added.

"Yeah, they might not believe two old geezers could even do that," Ben chuckled.

"They're going to want our information since his head injury could be the result of a crime. We have to try to get away before they ask."

"OK. We dump and run. Got it. I wonder how many pills it would take to knock out a guy this size." Ben opened the door and went in to explain the situation while Fitz stayed in the car just in case Victor tried to bolt. A surge of panic hit when he realized Victor still had the zip-ties on his wrists. He hurried to get them cut off.

Ben returned, leading two men with a gurney. One of the two, whose name badge read "Stan," opened the door.

"That's a big dude," Stan said. "I hope he can stand."

"We think he passed out on the way," Ben said.

Stan shook Victor but got no response. After an expletive he said, "OK, Rick. Let's do this." They managed to lift Victor onto the gurney.

"Uh, oh. Head injury. Let's move!" Stan and Rick took off with Victor on the gurney, leaving Fitz and Ben standing by the car.

Watching them hurry away, Ben said, "That was easy. I believe that's our cue to leave." They wasted no time in getting into the car and driving away.

Ben pulled into the Waffle House parking lot and scanned the area for a suitable place to drop the phone. "It's a shame I don't have Snickers with me. She would have provided good cover for wandering around in the grass."

Fitz finished wiping prints off the phone with his handkerchief, checked the doorway into the restaurant, rolled down the window, and tossed the phone onto the grass. "Let's go."

CHAPTER 32

As Ben pulled into the Walmart parking lot, Fitz said, "Turn off your lights. They might be sleeping."

Ben pulled by the line of cars and backed in next to Fitz's old Highlander. Everyone was still and quiet. "I think sleeping's a good idea," Ben suggested. "How about two hours? It's four forty-four, so I'll set an alarm for six forty-five."

"Perfect. I could use a nap." Fitz quietly moved to his car, let the seat back, and petted Buffett, who settled onto his lap. He had learned to sleep fast while in the army, and he successfully employed that skill.

A crowd of people were in a room when Fitz walked in. *A funeral parlor?* He didn't recognize anyone there. Assuming he must be there for the deceased, he made his way to the coffin. Sharon was lying there. *She looks so peaceful.* She smiled, and Fitz's heart warmed. *She's not dead!* She reached and patted him on the hand. "It's OK," she whispered. Her features became still as death.

A knock on the window startled Fitz awake. He puzzled over the dream as he nudged Buffett out of his lap and opened the door.

"Sorry I startled you," Ben said.

"No problem. I was having an odd dream."

"What was it about?"

"I don't want to talk about it," Fitz said. "Did you have any inspiration on how to catch this witch?"

"Not a one. How about you?"

"Nope. I wonder if she has figured out her hit man is out of commission."

*   *   *   *   *

"We need an alternate plan in case Victor fails," Crystal stated. "What can we do if they get away again?"

"Even worse, what if he catches them and brings them here?" Shannon asked.

Crystal's mouth dropped open. "Surely he wouldn't. He knows better than that ... doesn't he?"

"I guess we'll find out."

Crystal's nerves frayed as she waited to hear from Victor after sending him to the location of Fitz's phone. She checked her phone. "It's been thirty minutes since we called him."

"Maybe he's disposing of the bodies," Shannon suggested.

"I don't dare call him. It might give him away."

"We need to just wait. He'll call when he's ready." Shannon said.

"Unless they somehow capture him. Then what?"

"I suppose it could have been a trap," Shannon said.

Her comment prompted Crystal to resume pacing. *I hadn't considered the possibility of its being a trap. That's what I pay Victor for.* "Surely Victor considered that possibility."

"Surely he did."

The waiting dragged on. "It's four forty-five. He's had an hour. I'm calling." Crystal dialed Victor's number.

After five rings a strange voice answered, "Hello?"

Crystal's eyes widened, and she held the phone away, looking at it as if that would give her answers. "It's not Victor," she mouthed to Shannon.

Recovering, Crystal barked into the phone, "Who is this? You're not the person I called."

"No, ma'am. I heard the phone ringing and found it lying in the grass. I figured the person who lost it might be calling."

"Where are you?"

"I'm at the Waffle House on Limestone Parkway."

"Thank you for answering my call. Would you mind just leaving the phone with the staff? I'll let my friend know where it is when I find him."

Crystal disconnected the call. "Well, that's a predicament. Victor either dropped his phone, or they managed to take him."

"I'm betting he dropped it. How could they have known he was at the Waffle House?" Shannon asked.

"Could they have been tracking his phone while we were tracking them? I really don't like these people," Crystal fumed.

"We don't know if Victor is still functioning or dead. I say we plan as though he were out of commission."

"OK. What next?"

Shannon didn't respond. She had gone back to watching the security videos, studying the faces carefully so she could identify them if need be. That's when she noticed something she hadn't picked up on before.

*   *   *   *   *

"Shall we wake the others?" Ben asked.

"The sun will rise soon. Let them sleep till then. I'll start the coffee."

Ben stretched. "Good grief! The store is already open, and a few shoppers have arrived."

"Yeah. It's a busy place. It used to be open all night," Fitz said as he pulled water out of the back.

"Come on, Snickers. Let's go do your business."

Katía's car door opened, and she got out. The braids she had used to tame her hair had slipped a bit. "Good morning."

"I don't know if there's much good about it," Ben said.

"Sure there is. There is always something good. This is the day that we stop an evil woman from doing her crimes. Plus, we will soon have coffee." She zipped her jacket against the chill.

The first touch of pink showed in the sky. "I'm glad we can count on the sun rising," Ben said. "It never fails."

"I don't know if I have enough granola bars for everyone," Fitz said, rummaging through his food supplies after having put the water on to boil.

"I'm on it," Ben said and started toward the store.

"Use cash," Fitz called to him. Buffett was nosing around. "This is my food. Yours is in the back floorboard," Fitz said before giving him an ear scratch and closing the lift gate.

"I had an idea for catching Crystal," Katía announced.

Turning his eyes from the pot of water, Fitz asked, "What is it?"

"What if we get Zee to go and ask to buy drugs from her?"

"Suppliers usually don't sell directly to clients," Fitz answered. "She would probably act offended that he would even suggest such a thing."

"I see. What are we going to do, then? So far we look like the criminals."

"Yeah," Fitz said tugging on his beard. "I hope Victor didn't die."

As if he knew they were talking about him, Zee got out of his car and took King for a walk.

Victoria and Alejandro emerged from their car, and Victoria hurried over to Fitz and grabbed him in a hug. Fitz's eyes widened and his back stiffened. He grimaced.

"You saved my life twice. I am so grateful," Victoria said.

Fitz patted her back with one hand. "You're welcome," was all he came up with.

Zee moseyed up with King. "Mornin'. You look like your brain is about to explode."

"I'm trying to come up with a way to get this mad woman arrested," Fitz said.

"That's easy. All we need is for one of her workers to testify against her. Well, maybe two or three workers," Zee suggested.

"I bet they're all undocumented, so they'd be risking deportation if they came forward. That's got to be how she controls them," Katía said.

"I don't want to leave my family," Victoria said. "I just have come to be with them again."

"What if one of us goes to work for her?" Zee asked. "I could clean houses."

"I don't think you're her type, but I am," Luna offered.

"She knows you're with us, so that won't work," Katía observed. "Besides, that would take too long. We need something that will work today."

"Breakfast, anyone?" Ben asked, walking up with bags of juice and granola bars.

The pot of water had begun to boil, so Fitz served the first round of coffee while the rest of the crew dug into breakfast, except for Sofía, who was still asleep.

Fitz knelt to start another pot of coffee. *There has to be a way to catch this woman. I wonder if Victor would turn on her. I hope I didn't kill him with that whack to the head.*

CHAPTER 33

It was 7:22am when they finished breakfast and settled in to sipping coffee in the Walmart parking lot, brains churning in hopes the caffeine would fuel an idea to expose Crystal's crimes.

"There just has to be a way to link her to the drugs and Victoria's abduction that doesn't involve deportation," Ben said.

"You know, there was an article in the paper a week or so ago about a Latina woman's body being discovered. I wonder if Crystal is behind that," Katía said.

"Ooh, that's spooky," Luna replied. "Hey, Zee, could I borrow your phone?"

"Sure," Zee answered, handing it over.

"I want to see what Crystal is up to this morning."

"How are you going to do that? I wouldn't advise calling her," Fitz cautioned.

"You'd be surprised how much you can discover on social media. People will put anything on there," Luna said.

The others watched while Luna logged into her account and searched for Crystal Samson.

Katía asked Victoria, "How were your co-workers able to steal the pills?"

"They said it was easy. Clients keep them just lying around. They would even ask the workers to bring them a pain pill," Victoria answered.

After finding her, Luna pulled up Crystal's page and scanned for entries. "There's nothing here since three days ago. Let me see if there's a Sparkles page."

Fitz noticed the color drain from Luna's face as she read. *That can't be good.*

Holding the phone out, Luna said, "This is cryptic, and I think she is talking to us."

Fitz waited as they passed the phone around. When it got to him, he noticed the post was entered five minutes ago. It read, "Today promises to be a big day here at Sparkles. We've had some competitors snooping around and causing problems lately. I recently discovered one of my workers leaked information. I'll put an end to that problem right now. There should be a live and let live attitude between competitors, don't you think? Nevertheless, I always win at chess."

"That sorry dog," Fitz said as he handed the phone on to Ben. "I think she is threatening to kill one of her workers if we don't back off." Anger boiled, and he popped M&Ms into his mouth without even counting them.

"That's what it sounds like to me, too," Ben said after finishing the post. "Cruella Crystal is nastier than I thought."

"I guess it's back to the venue," Katía said.

"I doubt she would hide her there," Ben replied. "Unless she was laying a trap for us. If she expects us to go there, she will have a crew ready to take us out."

"I really don't want to give her the pleasure of doing that," Zee said.

Ben chuckled. "I agree totally."

"Still, we have to do something," Katía said. "I just wish I knew what that something was."

Fitz wandered away from the group, trying to focus. *I see two possibilities. One is that with her hit man down, she has taken matters into her own hands, in which case she'll hide this person in a different place. The second is that she has procured other people to do her dirty work and could set a trap like Ben said. What to do about it, though? Options. We need options. I need more M&Ms.*

"Hey, Fitz," Ben called. "Come back and see what you think of this idea."

Fitz, surprised by how far he had wandered, hurried back to the group.

"Luna suggested we respond to the post and say we'll give up if she returns the worker to us. Of course, we would have to phrase it a little more delicately," Ben explained.

"No. I'm not letting that woman get away with what she is doing," Fitz replied.

"What if it's just a ruse to lure us in? At least we could find that out," Katía said.

"Given her recent track record, I think she means it."

"Oh, no!" Katía's hand went to her mouth. "What if she saw María slip me the note in the parking lot? I bet they took her prisoner."

Silence settled over the group with the realization that what Katía said was probably true.

"Why do people always have to get abducted?" Zee groaned.

"If Crystal had Victor murder the woman mentioned in the paper, then I don't think María has a chance. She won't hesitate to kill her," Ben observed.

Fitz tugged his beard. "The only difference is her hired killer is out of commission; at least I hope he is. Would she have the gall to do the killing herself?"

"I think our first order of business is to rescue María. Then we can worry about getting Crystal arrested," Katía said. "I can't stand the thought of her being in that woman's clutches." She shuddered.

"I understand," Luna said, wrapping an arm around Katía.

"Yeah. Me, too," Zee said. "Being held against your will ain't fun. I just hope she has better accommodations than we did."

Fitz spoke up. "OK, we need to cool our jets. First of all, we don't know for sure that she has abducted anyone.

Secondly, if she has, we don't know that it's María. I don't suppose anyone has María's number, do they?"

"No, we didn't get that chummy," Luna answered.

"Oh! Helen should have it!" Katía brightened. "I could get it from her." Katía's phone was in her hand in an instant.

She was about to hit the power button when Ben said, "Stop. You'll alert Crystal to our location. Use Zee's phone."

"I don't know her number by heart. I need to turn on the phone to get it." She pressed the power button. "It will just be on for a second, then I'll turn it right back off. Get your phone ready, Zee."

Fitz wasn't paying attention, having drifted back to the dream at the funeral home. *It was so real. I wish she would just get up out of that coffin and come back to me.*

CHAPTER 34

Expletives chased the purse that Crystal threw to the chair after checking her makeup. "Where is Victor? Why was his phone at Waffle House? This should be over by now!" She stomped her foot.

"Calm down. Panicking won't help," Shannon said. "Something happened. I'm guessing they got the jump on Victor. Maybe it was a trap." She kept her eyes on the screen of the computer in Crystal's office, scanning in hopes one of the phones would signal a location. They had moved from Crystal's house to be ready for the work day and to lure María into their trap.

"Any response to the social media post?"

"You got three likes."

"If their phones are off, there's a slim chance they would see it. Do we know anyone who could take Victor's place?"

Crystal didn't like the look Shannon gave her before responding with, "I don't hang around with that type of people."

Walking to the chair into which she had thrown her purse, Crystal pulled out a Sig Sauer P365 and made sure it was loaded, even though she knew it was.

"Getting nervous?" Shannon asked.

Crystal's eyes spat fire back. "Are you armed?"

"Yes."

"We might have to take matters into our own hands."

"This is getting out of control. We need to focus on negotiating the trade," Shannon said.

"Do you really think that releasing that woman will buy their silence?" Crystal protested. "The only way this ends is if they're all silenced permanently."

"I think being up all night is wearing on us. Why don't you go home and get some sleep? I'll manage things here and let you know as soon as anything comes up."

"Like I'm going to sleep right now. Have you lost your mind? As soon as the workers are gone we have to move this one to the storage unit. I need her alive a little longer," Crystal said, referring to María, who was sitting across the room with her mouth taped shut and eyes wide with terror.

*　*　*　*　*

Zee handed his phone over to Katía after entering the number she read off to him. She cringed as she hit dial, knowing Helen was a late sleeper. After six rings it went to voicemail.

Katía tried to steady her voice as she said, "Hey, Helen. It's Katía. I was wondering if you had María, your housecleaner's, number. I'd like to get in touch with her. Please give me a call at this number…" She looked at Zee with questioning eyes, and he shrugged his shoulders. "My phone is out of commission, so I'm using a friend's phone. He can't remember his number, so just call back on the number associated with this voicemail."

Handing the phone back to Zee, she said, "I was afraid she wouldn't answer. She's not usually up before nine."

"Ooh! I've got it!" Luna said, mustering some excitement through her fatigue.

"Got what?" Ben asked.

"I know how we can respond to Crystal's post."

"Do you care to share?" Ben asked.

"How does this sound? 'It looks like a stalemate. You have something the competitor really wants, and they have something you need. It is unlikely either of you will blink.'"

Luna's excitement had drawn Fitz back in. "How does responding to her post help the situation?"

"It opens the avenue for dialogue. We could learn more about what she's planning," Katía said. "It also gives us a chance to talk her down and convince her to give herself up."

"Fat chance of that happening," Fitz said. "Do you realize how much prison time she'll be facing, especially if that murder is tied to her?" Fitz answered.

"What about the office manager? Maybe we could get her to turn on the boss to save her own hide," Ben suggested.

"That has possibilities," Fitz replied. "We just don't know how deeply she's involved. If she's just on the fringe and it's mostly Crystal and Victor, then we might have some leverage. What we would really need is a prosecutor who could offer a deal of lesser charges for cooperation."

"Maybe we should just call in an anonymous tip to get the venue searched. If they find anything, surely our testimony would help lead a path to Crystal," Ben said.

"Crystal has too many options that would lead to a jury's being uncertain about her guilt. She can claim it was all Victor's doing. She can also claim we planted the drugs since she has evidence we broke into her place. We still need to find something that ties her directly to this mess," Fitz argued.

"You realize we're in the proverbial pickle then, right?." Ben noted.

"I say we storm her office. If we don't find María there, then move on to her house," Zee suggested. "I'm tired of just waiting around."

"In a couple of hours I should hear back from Helen, and we can call to see if María answers," Katía reminded the group.

Fitz's spine tingled and he stiffened. "You mean you turned your phone on?"

The crack of a gun and the explosion of Ben's windshield punctuated his question.

"Behind the cars!" Fitz shouted, pulling out his Beretta as he hurried for cover. Another shot whizzed by over the top of his car. "Stay down," he said as he peeked around the car looking for the shooter.

He spotted a dark colored Camry four lanes over. Crystal sat in the passenger seat, handgun aimed in their direction. He aimed his pistol at her head but couldn't bring himself to take the shot. He fired into the back door, then yelled, "You need some target practice. My next shot goes through your head, Crystal."

The Camry took off, zooming out of the parking lot.

"I see they were still monitoring our phones," Ben said.

"Yeah, and we have to find another spot to hide," Fitz answered.

"Guys, I'm sorry I turned on my phone even after you told me not to," Katía said.

Fitz squelched the rising anger and decided it was best to say nothing.

"Where can we park a bunch of cars without drawing suspicion?" Carlos asked.

"Let's go to the park," Luna suggested.

"She's seen us there," Zee noted.

"Actually, I was thinking Longwood Park. We should be fine for the day, then we'll have to figure out something for tonight."

"I hope we're done with this by tonight," Zee said.

"I'll have to stay here till I get my windshield repaired," Ben moaned, looking over his car.

"Let's move it to the park or you'll have to answer to the police. I'm sure someone called them," Fitz pointed out.

"I can't drive it like this," Ben said. "I'd be eating bugs."

"Just drive slow and pretend you're on a motorcycle," Zee said. "I've done that before. It's kind of fun."

Ben gave Zee an "I can't believe you just said that" look.

"Let's go, then," Fitz said. He heard sirens wailing as he turned out of the Walmart parking lot. *It looks like the gunfire drew some attention. I hope they got Shannon's tag number. What if they got our tag numbers?*

CHAPTER 35

The five cars lined up in parking spaces at Longwood Park, which was on the lake just a short way from Walmart. A couple of runners passed by as they were getting out of the cars. Fitz gave Buffett an ear scratch before joining the others. They had gathered in a group by the time Ben pulled into the parking lot, having driven slowly to get there.

"I don't believe I want to turn this in to my insurance company," Ben said. "I need to find one of those companies that comes out and replaces windshields on site." He set his computer on the hood of the Outback.

Fitz scrunched up his eyes. "What good is the computer going to do you here? ... unless you have a cellular connection."

"Of course I have a cellular connection," Ben replied, booting up the computer.

Fitz's mind started churning with possibilities of what the computer might help them do.

"I say we claim one of the picnic tables under the pavilion," Luna suggested.

Sofía, who had been rudely awakened by the gunfire, said, "I want to go home."

Victoria slid her arm around her. "You just saw how dangerous this woman is. We have to stay hidden, mi amor."

Fitz stayed back with Ben while the others walked to the pavilion. "I think we need to pay this witch a visit."

"Are you nuts?" Ben said. "I guess you are nuts, but that still seems a bad idea. You'd just be asking for a shoot-out."

"Do you have any better ideas? If we can get to her and convince her to tell us where the drugs are, then we can call in the police."

Ben scratched his head. "I don't think she is going to cooperate. Besides, we'd be the ones ending up in jail for kidnapping and breaking into her property. Not to mention the fact that you put a bullet into her car."

"Yeah, I probably shouldn't have done that. I guess you noticed the police arriving as we left."

"I did. I had just turned onto the road when I saw the lights. I'm glad they couldn't see my windshield." Ben looked sadly at the gaping hole where the windshield used to be.

"So what are we going to do?"

Fitz puzzled at the grin forming on Ben's face. "What if we pay Victor a visit at the hospital?" Ben said.

"Why would we do that?"

"We might convince him to turn on Crystal. If he cooperates with helping us find the drugs, we'll promise a lenient sentence."

"We can't promise that."

"True, but he doesn't know that," Ben said.

"He has probably murdered at least one person. I don't think he'll cooperate."

"It depends on how doped up he is."

"Or how bad his head injury is," Fitz replied. "Maybe that is a possibility. You find a windshield repair place, and I'll tell the others what we're planning."

By the time Fitz returned, Ben had located an auto glass shop and arranged a repair. "They'll be here at one o'clock," he informed Fitz.

"I hope you don't mind a cat in your lap," Fitz said.

"That's fine, but I don't think Snickers will fit. I'll see if one of the others will watch her while we're gone."

"I already thought of that," Fitz said as Luna came walking up.

"I'm reporting for dog duty," she said.

On the way to the hospital, Ben asked, "Do you think Crystal has discovered that Victor's out of commission?"

"I'm sure she's figured it out. That's probably why she came gunning for us."

"We're lucky she's a bad shot."

"Or she missed on purpose."

"Why would she do that?" Ben asked.

"She might have been trying to frighten us off," Fitz replied.

"At least we're getting to her. The woman is coming unhinged. Now, exactly how are we going to approach our dear friend Victor?"

"I have no idea," Fitz replied.

They entered the Emergency Room and stopped at the desk. "We're here to see Victor Palfrey," Ben announced.

Fitz stuffed his hands in his pockets and scanned the waiting room, feeling exposed since he had to leave the Beretta in the car.

The woman at the desk finally responded. "He's no longer here."

Fitz stiffened, and his eyes met Ben's. "What do you mean? He was in such bad shape a couple of hours ago," Ben replied.

"Apparently a little Narcan was all he needed, then he checked himself out. They thought he might have a mild concussion, but he refused to be evaluated."

"Who picked him up?" Fitz asked, feigning the puzzled friend.

"He said a friend was coming to get him and walked out."

"Well, OK then. That Narcan must be powerful stuff."

"It is if that's what you need," the woman said and refocused on her computer screen.

Fitz and Ben returned to Fitz's Highlander. Buffett was asleep in the back seat.

"At least it wasn't my whack on the head that did it," Fitz said.

"I wish it had been. He'd probably still be here."

"It looks like it's back to stalemate," Fitz said.

"Maybe we should call in the police and let them sort it out," Ben said, petting Buffett as he settled into his lap.

"You're probably right. I just think there's a big chance Crystal will get away scot-free."

"I don't know what else we can do," Ben said.

"When we get back to the park, let's see if the others have any ideas. If not, I guess we call the police."

CHAPTER 36

Fitz sensed something was off as he pulled into Longwood Park. The cars were all just where they'd been. It just seemed too… quiet.

"Something's not right," he said.

"They're just down at the pavilion."

"I don't see them. Something's not right." He parked and hurried to get out, retrieving the Beretta from under the seat.

After convincing Buffett to get out of his lap, Ben hopped out, too. He scanned the park, especially down by the lake. "You're right. I don't see them."

"What's that?" Fitz walked down the sidewalk about a fifty feet. Four drops of blood stained the sidewalk. "He found them."

Looking up, Fitz caught a glimpse of a head pulling behind the corner of the building that housed the bathrooms. His hand instinctively went for the Beretta.

The face peeked out again. It was Alejandro. He hurried their way. "We took Sofía for Chik-Fil-A, and when we came back the rest were gone, except for Zee."

Zee came limping up, leading King. "I was in the bathroom cleaning up and heard gun shots. By the time I got out, some monster of a man was loading them into a Hummer."

"Who was bleeding?" Fitz asked.

"I'm guessing Katía. She was holding her arm funny and looked to be in pain," Zee answered.

"How long ago did it happen?" Ben asked.

"I'd guess about ten minutes," Zee said.

"We have to get out of here. They'll be back," Fitz said, searching his mind for a place to hide. *It needs to be far enough away from here that they can't guess.* After three pulls of his beard, he said, "Let's go to the Kroger lot on Jesse Jewell Parkway. That should get us through the day.

"But they're coming to fix my windshield at one," Ben griped, taking Snickers' leash from Sofía.

"You can send them the new address when we get there. Let's move." Fitz hurried the Lopez family into their car. "Just take your time and wear sunglasses," he said to Ben.

"I'll see you when I see you," he replied.

*   *   *   *   *

"You got blood on my Hummer! I should have just killed you at the park!" Victor griped as he dragged Katía out of the car, taking no care to avoid hurting the arm his bullet had grazed.

Katía groaned as pain shot up and down her left arm. The blood seemed to have slowed down at least. With Victor having snatched her gun, she saw no way to get them out of this mess.

Victor waved his pistol like a wild man, growling, "Don't move till I say so."

Shannon was unlocking the door to a run-down self-storage unit. *Apparently we're going in there,* Katía thought.

"Shannon has a brilliant mind, doesn't she?" Crystal gloated. "It was her idea to shoot out a windshield and run you to a less crowded spot so Victor could bring you in. The guy with the long beard will pay for putting a hole in her door, though."

Shannon raised the garage-style door, revealing an empty space with the exception of a port-a-potty in one corner. "I hope you enjoy your new home till we get the others and figure out exactly how to dispose of you," she sneered.

"It has all the comforts of home," Crystal said, stepping forward and patting Katía on the hand she held over her wound.

Katía winced but refused to let out the groan.

"In you go," Shannon directed, and Victor resumed waving his gun in the direction of the unit.

Katía glared at him as she led Luna and Carlos into the unit. She noticed movement in the dark corner as the door began to shut behind them. *I bet that's María.* Hopelessness pressed down on Katía as the door clanked shut, leaving them in darkness.

Crystal called to them. "You're welcome to scream all you want. I own this place, and there won't be any one else coming by to hear." The sound of car doors shutting was followed by the retreat of the engines.

"María? Is that you?" Katía called in the darkness.

"Sí. She grabbed me when I came in for work this morning. She said I would be here till I helped catch you."

"I hate to say it, but I don't believe she has any intention of letting us go," Katía replied. "Are you OK?"

"Sí, but I'm cold."

Loud clanking rang out. Carlos was shaking the door, pushing and pulling. Next he kicked it five times. It dented but held. "We have to get out of here," he said.

Light seeped around the edges of the door just enough for Katía to see when Carlos stepped in front of it. "Check the other side to see if you can find the lock," she said.

"It was a padlock on the outside, remember," Luna answered.

"Do you remember which side it was on?" Carlos asked.

"It was on the left as we were coming in. I watched Shannon unlock it.

The light partly disappeared on the right of the door frame. "You might want to cover your ears," Carlos said. He kicked five more times but didn't break through.

"Let me help," Katía said, moving beside him. "Let's do one, two, three, kick." Each kick sent sharp pains through Katía's arm.

Even after twelve tries, the lock didn't give, but a sliver of light appeared in the panel. "I need a breather," Katía said, hope growing with the pain. A fresh trickle of blood ran down her arm. She could hear Carlos's heavy breathing.

"Let's all kick," Sofía suggested.

With Katía holding her arm and huffing and puffing, the others lined up. "One, two, three, kick," Carlos led the attack. With ten more kicks, the crack in the panel widened just a hair.

"Everybody take a break," Katía directed. "Let's catch our breath and try again."

Once everyone had regained steady breathing, they lined up. "You hit just to the right of the crack and I'll hit to the left," Katía said to Carlos.

"OK," Carlos said and resumed the count.

They continued kicking in bursts of ten, but the door held. The crack grew no more. Katía sat gingerly on the floor, holding her arm. "I feel lightheaded."

"Carlos, do you have a handkerchief? We need to tie up her wound," Luna said.

Carlos produced his handkerchief, and Luna knelt beside Katía. "Put your index and middle fingers on each side of the wound so I can find it." Folding the handkerchief into a strip, she wrapped it around Katía's arm. There was barely enough to tie it, but she managed.

Katía leaned her head back against the wall, pain mixing with wooziness. "I never thought my life would end in a storage unit."

CHAPTER 37

Fitz paced the lane of the Kroger parking lot, his pulse pounding at the thought of Katía being injured and in the hands of that brute. M&Ms weren't helping. *This wouldn't have happened if I hadn't been so stubborn. I should have called in the police to start with. What have I done?*

He stomped along the row of cars, and Katía's image morphed into Sharon. A tear warmed his cheek. *I'm sorry, sweetheart. I can't visit with you right now. I have to figure out how to save someone.*

He was sure he heard Sharon say, "That's what I love about you. You care so much for people. You can figure this out." Stopping, he looked around, almost expecting to see her. "I wish you were still here. I would have left the service and married you so that we could have had more time together," he said aloud.

"It's not too late," returned from the void. Fitz looked around puzzled for a second before his mind brought him back to the present. *I wish it weren't too late.*

Shaking his head, he steered his brain back to figuring out how to save the others. He turned and walked back, the sun warming his face as the cold temperature of the night eased its grip. When he reached his car, he felt tired. He got in and sat down, and Buffett hopped into his lap.

"I don't know how to get out of this mess, Buffett. Katía is wounded, and I don't know where they've taken her."

"Meow." Buffett rubbed his chin.

"I miss Sharon, too."

Buffett rubbed his chin again and purred.

"I know I have you, and I'm grateful. Grief is a hard thing to shake. I can't believe it's still eating at my soul." He leaned his head back. While trying to think, he drifted off to sleep.

A tap on the window dragged Fitz back to consciousness. Ben was standing there. "Wake up, Sleeping Beauty."

Fitz pushed the door open. Ben smiled wide. "Do I have any bugs in my teeth?"

"I don't see any. You must have kept your mouth shut."

"Good. They're coming here to fix the windshield. Have you had any groundbreaking ideas on how to get the others back?"

"Not a one," Fitz answered, worry escalating.

"She'll kill them, I'm afraid."

"I don't think she will until she has us, too. She needs them for bait. Do you think it's time to call in the police?"

Ben scratched his neck. "What would you do if the police showed up at your door and you were holding four people hostage?"

"I'd lie, then get rid of them as soon as I could," Fitz answered.

"Exactly. I think they'll be in more danger if the police go poking around."

"Is there anything you can do with the computer that would help us?"

"I can locate her cell phone. At least we'd know where she is. I could keep an eye on our dear friend, Victor, too."

"I doubt Victor picked up his phone from Waffle House," Fitz said.

"Oh, yeah," Ben replied.

"Can you tell where she has been?"

"No. It will just show me her current location."

Fitz ran his fingers through his long beard. "We have to think like criminals. Where would I hide a whole group of people? Certainly not at my house."

"Probably not at the venue, either," Ben suggested. "One of those self-storage units?"

"That would be too risky. Someone could happen by and hear them."

"True."

"Maybe she owns another property. Is there any way to find that out?"

"I can snoop around," Ben said and turned to get the computer out of his car. Snickers had her front feet on the hood, head sticking out of the glassless window. "I forgot that you could get out, girl. Actually, I'm going to sit back here so I can see the screen better." He climbed into the back seat. Fitz went around and got in on the other side.

While Ben was booting up the computer, Victoria called, "Anybody hungry?" She held up a bag. Alejandro and Sofía followed with Starbucks coffees.

"I am definitely up for food," Ben replied.

Victoria pulled out muffins from the store's bakery and handed out napkins. Ben opened the cupholder between the seats and continued with the computer. "If I were a conceited, evil woman, where would I mention the properties I own?"

"We didn't notice anything on her website," Fitz said.

"I'd brag about it on social media," Sofía said.

"Brilliant," Ben replied. "Let me see if I can find her."

"I think Luna found one account for Crystal and another for Sparkles," Fitz added.

Having located Crystal's profile, Ben began scrolling through posts. "This could take a while."

"There is no telling how long ago she might have purchased other properties," Fitz said.

"I don't have anything better to do than scroll through this witch's posts," Ben added.

Scrolling through the posts, he said, "This woman thinks a lot of herself. Most of these are of her at big, fancy events."

"You're looking for something like an announcement of a property purchase," Fitz prompted.

"I know that."

"I don't think you'll find anything," Zee said. "If I was usin' a property to hide folks in, I wouldn't broadcast it to the world."

"That's true," Fitz replied, "But you're not as egotistical as she is."

"I think Zee's right. I'm not seeing anything except her at fancy events or with fancy people," Ben said.

"Time is not on our side. We have to find them. I don't know how badly Katía is wounded," Fitz said.

"I just hope they didn't go straight and kill them," Zee said.

A jolt of angst pierced Fitz's heart. *What if that's true? I won't be able to live with myself if they're dead. They can't be dead.* Another jolt hit. This time it was enlightening.

"I know what I have to do," Fitz said.

CHAPTER 38

Ben looked over from the computer. "Do you care to share what it is you have to do?"

"I'm going to her office and turn myself over to her," Fitz announced.

"That's a brilliant idea," Ben replied. "Then it will just be Zee and me to rescue everyone."

"That's the plan. I'll go to the office and demand their release. When Victor hauls me to where ever they are holding the others, you'll be following."

"And what if I lose you?"

"Don't do that. If you use Zee's car, they won't recognize it, and you'll be able to follow closer."

"If we do manage to follow you to the place where the others are, then what? If we pull up, he'll probably start shooting, starting with you."

"If you drive past where he stops you can come back after he leaves and get us out."

"I can't see how anything could possibly go wrong with this plan," Ben snarked.

Fitz stroked his beard, looking from Ben to Zee and back to Ben. "If you have a better idea, I'm all ears. Otherwise, I'm heading to the Sparkles office. You can trail me or not. That's your choice." He turned and walked around his car to get in.

"Hold on a minute. You don't even know if they're at the office. Let's see if I can locate their phones first," Ben said.

"I don't have time for that. Let's go." Fitz started to sit down, then poked his head back out. "If I die, take care of Buffett for me."

He turned right out of the parking lot, heading toward the Sparkles office. As he drove, he got angrier and angrier thinking about the fact that they just tossed Katía in a room somewhere and left her bleeding. *They'd just let her die a slow and agonizing death rather than tend to her wounds. I should just show up and shoot all of them... But then no one would know where the others are.*

Fitz wasn't sure whether he was more relieved or anxious when he pulled into the Sparkles parking lot and all three vehicles were there. On his way to the front door, he stopped to look at the bullet hole in Shannon's door.

Entering the front door, he saw no one. A sign pointed upstairs to the offices. *I think I'll take a look around down here for the drugs. That should get their dander up.*

He went into what looked like a supply room and started opening closets and looking through bins. It wasn't long till he heard, "Hands up."

Turning to see Victor in the doorway, gun drawn, Fitz said, "You're just the person I was looking for. I thought I'd find you down here."

"Up the stairs. Crystal wants a word with you before you die."

"A man of few words. I like that about you. I'm glad you survived your overdose. How's your head doing?"

Victor waved his gun toward the stairs, and Fitz complied. He found Crystal and Shannon waiting for him in Crystal's office.

Wrangling his nerves to project a calm façade, Fitz said, "Mornin', Crystal. Shannon."

Crystal's eyes spit darts. "You understand that you and your motley crew have to die for the trouble you've caused me. I will not let you take down my empire."

"Now, now. We don't have to get all drastic. Let's see if we can work something out."

"I don't see anything to work out except where to dump the bodies," Crystal responded.

"How about this? You let my friends go and just keep me. Does that work for you?"

"Don't be ridiculous."

"OK. I didn't think you'd go for that. Here's a better offer. You tell me where you're hiding the drugs, and I turn you over to the police to pay for the crimes you've committed."

Victor's punch to the side of his head caught Fitz off guard, and he staggered sideways. Recovering, he said, "That wasn't very neighborly of you, Victor."

"I have an offer for you," Crystal growled. "Tell me where the others are hiding, and Victor will kill you quickly. Otherwise there will be a lot of suffering involved first."

"Such a tempting offer. I don't see how I could refuse. I'll go consider it and be back in a couple of hours." He turned to leave, and Victor stepped in front of the door.

"Now, Victor. Play nice." He turned back to Crystal to find her aiming a pistol at him. Her hand was shaking and rage etched every line on her face.

Shannon stepped over and said quietly, "Not here. Someone will hear."

Crystal's lips curled in a smile laced with evil. "You know what to do, Victor. Extract the location of the others, then dump the body as usual."

Victor grabbed the collar of Fitz's shirt, nearly lifting him off the floor, and shoved him toward the door. "We're going for a ride."

"Aren't you forgetting something, Victor?" Shannon said.

Victor looked puzzled. "You want me to do it here?"

"No. His hands. Shouldn't you handcuff him?" Shannon suggested.

"I think the drugs are starting to affect your mind. You might need to cut back a little," Crystal said. "Don't screw this up."

Victor replied, "I want him to look normal walking to the car. Any passersby could get suspicious if his hands are tied."

Fitz noted the tinge of anger in Victor's voice. *I wonder if I could turn him against her.*

CHAPTER 39

Victor growled, "Take off your coat."

Fitz slid his arms out of his jacket. *I wonder why it took him this long to check for my weapon.*

As he was pulling the coat around from his back, Victor snatched his Beretta. "Any other surprises?" he asked.

"That shouldn't have been a surprise," Fitz scolded. "No, I don't have any other weapons."

"Don't move." Victor patted him down and pulled the phone from his pocket. "Let's go for a ride." He shoved Fitz toward the door.

Walking past his Highlander, Fitz noticed Buffett standing, paws on the dashboard, watching. *I should have left you with Victoria. At least you have food and water.* He reached the Hummer, and Victor opened the passenger door.

"You mean I get to ride in the front? That's kind of you."

"You'll see how kind I can be soon. Don't try to run. It'll be worse."

"Thanks for the warning." Fitz's mind churned to decide on a strategy to turn Victor against Crystal. *I might not have long.*

"You must have a nice set up here if she pays you enough to drive this," Fitz began. "How much does one of these cost?" He waited for a reply, but Victor sat stoically.

"I'd guess eighty to ninety thousand at least. You used to be able to buy a nice house for that."

"I'm glad you like to talk. You could save yourself some agony by just telling me where the others are hiding," Victor responded.

"Would it help if I told you I don't know? Everyone scattered after Crystal took that shot at us. By the way, why didn't she send you to shoot us down at Walmart? She totally missed. She'd have been better served had she sent a pro like you. I think she is trying to push you out and take over what she's had you doing. It would obviously save her a lot of money, and that's what is important to her."

Fitz glanced and noticed a slight narrowing of Victor's eyes. *It's working.*

"You know where they are, and soon you'll tell me," Victor said.

"I'm not a big fan of torture, so I'd tell you if I knew. When I left to come to the office, I told them to go somewhere else just so I couldn't betray them."

"Why did you come to the office? That was stupid. Good for us but stupid for you."

"I was hoping to talk some sense into your dense boss. She is setting herself up for life in prison. She is setting you up for the death penalty. You will get caught, you know.

Right now, she can blame it all on you and say she had nothing to do with it. That's why we didn't call the police. I wanted a chance to talk with her first. She's going to pin all this on you and walk away free. Is that what you want? I was just trying to help you out."

Fitz noticed Victor's glance in his peripheral vision. They passed the airport and turned right onto Queen City Parkway. Fitz looked over and noticed Victor's lips had curled into a slight smile. *That's not good.*

"Crystal is a nasty little critter," Victor said. "I'm not sure why I've put up with her this long. So you think you can help me get out of this?"

"If you cooperate with the investigation, I'm sure they'll give you a plea deal," Fitz said, taking the chance that now was the time to go for it.

"You're a funny little guy. I hate what I'm about to have to do to you."

Victor pulled into an old, condemned warehouse and parked by a door in the back. "Welcome to the party shack. We can make all the noise we want," he said with a grin.

Fitz noticed a motorcycle parked near the door. It was an off-road bike. "It looks like we have company," Fitz said.

"Maybe," Victor replied. He hurried around the car. He had donned a pair of gloves and drawn his gun by the time he opened Fitz's door.

"You've been such a pleasant soul that I'm going to let you walk into the building on your own," Victor growled.

"Is Crystal really worth all of this?"

"You have no idea what you're talking about. Now move. I want you inside before your friends arrive… Yes, they managed to keep up with us."

When Fitz hesitated, Victor grabbed his collar and propelled him inside the building. The door opened into a cavernous space, dimly lit by windows at the top. An assortment of pallets, conveyor belts, and old equipment littered the floor.

Victor hurried Fitz to the right and into what must have been an office suite at one time.

"You really don't want to do this," Fitz said. "It will only make your sentence worse."

"Like I said before, you have no idea what you're talking about. Hands, please."

Victor held zip-ties. When Fitz didn't comply, he whacked him in the head with the butt of his pistol, knocking Fitz to the ground.

"I only have about five minutes, so we don't have time to stall," Victor growled as he placed a knee on Fitz's back and zip-tied his hands. "I was going to let you sit in the chair, but this will work."

Producing a hunting knife, Victor said, "Where are the others hiding?" He didn't wait for an answer before slicing Fitz's shoulder. He cut the other shoulder. "Care to share?"

Fitz winced with the pain and hoped Ben and Zee would get there in a hurry. Then he remembered telling them not to come in until Victor left. His heart sank, but he came up with a stall tactic.

"What do you mean I don't know what I'm talking about?"

"Tell me what I want to know, and I'll answer that question." Victor dug the knife in about an inch between Fitz's ribs and twisted. The pain forced an agonizing groan.

"You liked that one, huh? We can do it again unless you want to tell me what I need to know."

Fitz had decided what he would tell Victor if it got to this point. "If you'll stop, I'll tell you."

Victor paused with the knife tip touching Fitz's side. "I'm waiting."

"We moved to the Home Depot lot out from the garden section."

The knife pierced his side and new pain scorched through his body. "Good try, but I'm not stopping till I believe you."

Fitz gasped and tried to roll away, but Victor pinned him down. "You're not going anywhere. I know that's a lie because you wouldn't stay so close by after we found your second spot."

"You could get out from under Crystal's thumb and start fresh. You don't have to do this." Fitz decided to try one more time.

"You have it all wrong, and since you'll be dead soon, I might as well tell you. Crystal isn't my boss. I'm hers. I'm an enforcer for the Cañería cartel. Hers is a small operation, but she has been faithful over the years, so we show her some love. I just happened to be here when you and your cronies decided to interfere. How fortunate for me. I am grateful for you taking me to the hospital, by the way. But it does make this task less pleasant for me."

Is he delusional from the opioids or being for real? Let me try this. "Interesting. How about sharing where you're holding my friends, too, since you're on a roll."

"Sure. They're in a storage unit on Atlanta Highway. That's the last place they will ever be. Now, one more chance. Where are the others?"

A loud clang caused both men to jump. Victor pulled his gun and raced to the window, scanning the building through the dingy glass. Fitz eyed the knife that Victor dropped in his haste. Apparently the glass was so dirty Victor couldn't see through it. He moved to the door and peered out.

"That must be who belongs to that motorcycle," Fitz suggested.

Victor didn't respond. He was focused on the threat. Fitz slid toward the knife. Victor glanced, noticed the knife, and scooped it up. "I'll finish with you in a minute."

Another clang drew Victor back to the door. He ducked, stepped through the doorway and hurried along the wall toward the noise. Fitz could see only the top of his head as he moved.

The crack of a gunshot caused Fitz to jump. A groan preceded four shots in a row coming from the direction in which Victor had moved. Another shot rang out from the opposite direction, followed by the sound of a door opening. Footsteps signaled someone coming. *Whoever's coming can't be any worse than Victor.*

Ben's face appeared in the window. The sound of a motorcycle penetrated the wall, then it screamed away. Ben walked through the doorway. "How badly are you hurt?"

"I hope I'll live. I thought I told you to wait until he left. I almost had him."

"I see that. It's a good thing I'm a bad listener."

"What if he comes back?"

"Zee is keeping an eye out. We need to get you to a hospital."

"There's no time for that. We have big problems." Fiz struggled, and Ben helped him to his feet.

"I don't guess he was kind enough to tell you where the others are being held."

The pain forced Fitz to speak in short phrases. "He did, and that's just… one of the big problems… Since I know where they are… he's probably on his way to kill them."

Ben started to wrap his arm around Fitz to help him walk, but Fitz caught his wrist in time. "He stuck a knife in my ribs."

"Oh, sorry. What's the other big problem?"

"He said he's an enforcer… for an international drug cartel."

CHAPTER 40

Fitz gingerly sat down in Ben's car, and Ben pulled out a first aid kit. "Were you a boy scout?" Fitz asked.

"Can I help it if I believe in being prepared? Pull up your shirt." Ben applied antibiotic ointment and bandages to the wounds. "Those are deep gashes. You're going to need stitches and antibiotics at least."

"We have to get to the… others before he does," Fitz said. "Zee see if you can find… any self-storage units on Atlanta Highway. And thank you… for rescuing me… It was getting brutal," Fitz managed, requiring four breaths. He leaned his head back and groaned.

"It looks like there's one down near Flowery Branch and one near Industrial Boulevard," Zee called from the back seat as Ben drove back toward town.

"It's probably the Industrial Boulevard one. It's closer to her office," Ben said.

Fitz grunted agreement. "Something doesn't add up… If this guy is part of an… international cartel, why would she have him… listed on her website?"

"Maybe he was lyin' to make himself look important," Zee replied.

"Why lie when he… was about to kill me?"

"Some folks just cain't help lyin' to make themselves look bigger than they are," Zee said.

"She might have listed him just in case anyone saw him at the office and wondered who he is," Ben suggested. "In which case, Victor Palfrey might not be his real name."

"That makes sense," Fitz said.

"Another question is why take off on the motorcycle and abandon the Hummer?" Ben asked.

"Maybe he thought you… had called the police, and… they'd be looking for the Hummer," Fitz replied.

"In a quarter of a mile you will arrive at your destination," the GPS app announced.

"I need to get to Buffett… right after we tend… to getting the others out," Fitz said.

"We need to get you to a hospital, too," Ben said. "You're struggling."

"There on the left," Zee called from the back seat.

Ben turned into the drive of a run-down looking self-storage facility. The entrance gate was padlocked.

"Great. It's locked," Fitz groaned.

"That's no problem," Ben said. "Are we sure this is the right place?"

"What do ya mean, no problem?" Zee asked. "I cain't break that chain."

"I have a cut-off tool in the back," Ben said.

Fitz couldn't believe his ears and gave him a look that said so.

"What? Can I help it if I'm prepared? I picked it up when I was packing."

"Where are you going to plug it in?" Zee asked.

"It's battery powered. And yes, I keep it charged," Ben answered.

He got out, opened the liftgate, instructed Snickers to stay put, and cut the chain. When he turned off the tool, they could hear muffled calls coming from one of the units. "That has to be them," he said.

With the gate opened, Ben hopped back into the car. "It sounded like they're in the middle row."

"How many guns do we have?" Fitz asked.

"Just one," Ben said.

"Can you shoot, Zee?" Fitz asked.

"I'm a good shot when I'm sober."

"Take the gun and… keep a look out while we find them."

"Luna! Katía!" Ben yelled, handing the gun to Zee.

"We're in here!" Luna's voice returned.

"Stay in the car, Fitz. We've got this." Ben hurried to the door from which the voice had come, cut off the padlock, and raised the door.

Fitz groaned as he got out of the car and walked toward the unit, holding both sides of his ribs. Luna had Katía's good arm around her shoulders and was helping her walk.

"What's wrong?" Fitz managed.

"I think she's lost too much blood," Luna answered.

Fitz's heart ached at the site of Katía hurting. "I'm sorry," he said, leaning forward against the pain.

"You don't look so good yourself," Katía replied.

"Who's that?" Ben asked as María walked out.

"This is María, the one who slipped Katía the note," Luna said.

"Nice to meet…," Ben said. Snickers interrupted, barking wildly. A couple of seconds later the sound of a motorcycle pierced the joyful reunion.

"He's here!" Fitz barked, adrenaline surging and pushing his pain down. "Where's the gun? Everyone back into the unit."

Zee pulled out Ben's gun. "I've got it."

"I need that. Get inside with the others."

Ben took the gun before Zee handed it to Fitz. "I think you need to get inside. I'm more fit for this right now."

Fitz turned to argue, and pain zinged both sides of his ribs. With a groan, he said, "Maybe you're right. Get behind the car for cover."

Ben was already crouching behind the hood. "Hurry up! Zee, pull the door down."

"You're going to have to kill him before he kills you," Fitz said.

"I know. Now get inside."

"Get ready. It's going to be dark when the door closes," Luna said as Zee pulled it down.

Fitz sat down next to Katía as the door banished the light.

"You OK?" Katía asked.

"I've been better."

"Me, too. I'm worried about Ben."

"Me, too."

The motorcycle sounded like it was at the entrance to the storage buildings when it stopped. *He probably realizes we're here since the gate was open. Now what will he do? Lord help Ben.*

Fitz heard the motorcycle slowly getting closer. His nerves tensed, and he had to work to avoid holding his breath. He wanted to yell out instructions to Ben but knew he had to trust that Ben could handle the situation. *Lord help him.*

Katía had leaned so that her shoulder was touching his. "He's got this," Fitz whispered to encourage her.

The motorcycle had stopped, the engine idling. *He's being cautious.* Fitz jumped at the sound of a gunshot, drawing a surge of pain. It was followed by four or five more shots, then the growl of the motorcycle as it zoomed away.

The door began to rise, and light jumped back into the room.

"We need to get out of here," Ben said while Fitz could still see only his knees. "Everybody in the car. Would someone mind sitting in the back with Snickers?"

"I'd love to, and María can join me," Luna said.

They all scrambled into the car, and Ben took off.

CHAPTER 41

Fitz's mind churned as Ben drove back to the Kroger parking lot. *What do we do now? We need to get Katía to a hospital. I need some pain medicine.* Ben's words broke through his thoughts. He was saying something about water.

"… water when we get back. If that doesn't help we're taking you to the ER."

"I'll be fine. I don't need to go to the ER. Fitz is the one we need to take," Katía responded, her voice sounding weak.

"We'll see," Ben said.

"I think we need to take you. You're too young for someone to have to help you walk," Fitz added.

"You're in worse shape than I am," she replied.

"If you two don't hush, I'm taking you both straight to the hospital," Ben said. "We'll do a better assessment when we get back to Kroger."

Fitz was sitting in the back seat next to Katía. Her head landed on his shoulder. He shook her gently, but she didn't wake up.

"I think Katía just passed out. We need to head straight to the ER," Fitz said.

"Got it," Ben said, and Fitz felt the car accelerate.

Pulling up to the emergency room entrance, Ben said, "I'll grab a wheelchair. Do you need one, too, Fitz?"

"I can walk. Let's just get Katía tended to." Fitz stayed put so Katía wouldn't fall over. When Ben returned with a wheelchair, he eased out of the seat trying to hold her up, but the pain was too much. "I can't hold her."

Ben reached in and put his hand on her shoulder. "I've got her. Just get out of the way. Carlos, would you grab her legs?"

Ben pulled her toward the edge of the seat and Carlos assisted as they set her into the wheelchair.

This will get the police involved since it's a gunshot wound, but I have to get her some help. Fitz walked on into the ER, not feeling so well himself.

As he got closer, he noticed Katía was holding her head up. "Are you OK?" he asked, touching her on the shoulder.

"I'm not feeling so good. How did we get here?"

"You passed out in the car," Fitz answered.

"Sir, could I see your Id and insurance card?" the woman at the desk asked. It took a second before Fitz realized she was talking to him.

"This is who we need to see about," he said, pointing toward Katía.

"I've already entered her into the system. You're next," the woman said. "Let me see those cards and tell me what's going on."

"Go on, Fitz. You might as well get treated since we're here," Ben encouraged.

Fitz grunted as he reached back for his wallet.

"Good. Luna and Carlos are staying here. I'm taking María and Zee back to the others and picking up Katía's purse. Behave and do what they tell you, Fitz."

After Fitz explained his wounds, the woman at the desk called out to a security guard, "Keep the police coming. We have two more attack victims."

"I'd rather not involve the police," Fitz said.

"Sorry, we're obligated by law to report gunshot wounds and other suspicious injuries. Please have a seat and you'll be called back soon."

Then the woman looked directly at Katía. "Ma'am, is this the man who shot you? Was it a domestic dispute?"

Katía shook her head. "No, he helped save me." She reached up and patted Fitz's arm.

"Please tend to her first. She's been passing out," Fitz said.

"Only once," Katía replied.

Carlos rolled Katía over to wait her turn.

As Fitz sat down near Katía, what the woman had said dawned on him. *Two more victims. That means Victor is here.*

Fitz told the others his suspicions, and Luna said, "Good. That will make it easier to catch the dog."

First, they called for Katía, and Luna rolled her over. Shortly after that, they called Fitz back, and Carlos went with him. The nurse, a thin blond thirty-something named Beth, settled Fitz into the bed and started an IV.

"The doctor will be in soon. If you need anything just push the call button," she said, picking up a little button on a cord. She hustled out of the room.

The doctor, a tall lanky man with short, tightly curled hair and a close-trimmed beard, popped in. "Hi, I'm Dr. Summerour. Let's have a look at you." He examined Fitz, had the nurse add antibiotics to the IV, and returned with a suture kit. "We need to stitch up those wounds."

Fitz winced as the doctor injected a local anesthetic around the wounds. After that, the stitching process wasn't too bad.

"I'm prescribing oral antibiotics for you to take in addition to the IV. I don't see any need to keep you, but I would like you to finish that bag of IV fluids before leaving. Do you have any questions?"

"No questions. I do appreciate your help," Fitz replied. He relaxed into the pillow as the doctor walked out. "Maybe we can get out of here before the police come," he said to Carlos. "Would you mind checking on Katía?"

Carlos left the room, and Fitz closed his eyes. He popped them back open at the sound of, "There's my problem child. I trust you're having a nice rest."

"I assume Victor called you," Fitz stated, glaring into Crystal's eyes.

"Yes. He's such a loyal puppy. I came to pay my final respects." She whipped out a syringe from her purse and injected something into his IV bag. "Sweet dreams," she grinned.

Fitz was frozen, unable to believe what she had just done. Then he kicked into gear and pulled the IV from his arm. "You're going to have a long time to repent of your sins when you're in prison for the rest of your life."

Crystal laughed and stepped forward. Picking up the suture needle, she stepped closer to the bed.

"Hospitals frown on people killing their patients, you know," Fitz said, readying himself for the attack.

The nurse popped in. "Here's your prescription. Make sure you get it filled on your way…" She stopped when she noticed the IV line dangling from the pole. "What have you done?"

"Beth, please get this woman out of here. She's trying to kill me," Fitz said.

Crystal turned so the little table was behind her and slid the suture needle back onto the table while saying, "I expect my alimony check within the next week." She turned and stormed out.

"That's not my ex-wife. She's an evil soul who injected some kind of poison into the IV bag."

He watched as the Beth's eyes narrowed and her lips pursed. *She's trying to decide if I'm delirious.* "I'm not making that up. Check the bag, and you'll find the needle hole."

"I think I need to speak with Dr. Summerour. I'll be right back."

Fitz plopped his head back onto the pillow and groaned with the surge of pain. "Katía!" He fought his way out of the bed, pain amplifying gravity. Once out in the hallway, he yelled, "Katía! Katía!"

Carlos emerged from a room. "She's over here."

Fitz hurried, the open-backed hospital gown flowing behind him. Rushing into the little treatment room, he asked, "Was Crystal here?"

"Yeah," Katía said, still sounding a bit faded. "She was talking all sweet and saying how she hated that Victor had harmed us."

Fitz pushed Carlos aside, stepped over Luna's feet, and shut off the flow regulator to stop the IV drip.

"Fitz, she needs the fluids," Luna protested.

"Crystal injected something into my IV bag. I'm sure it was poison," he replied.

"She did go over and look at the IV bag, but I didn't see her put anything in it."

"You wouldn't have, since she blocked your view. When I told the nurse she had done that to me, I could tell she thought I was crazy."

Beth stepped into the room, glared at Fitz, and said, "What are you doing in here? Get back to your room."

Fitz stood his ground and replied, "The woman who was in my room was in here, too. I believe she poisoned Katía's IV bag, too."

"Don't make me call security, Mr. Fitzgerald. I expect you to return to your room right now."

"I'm sorry, but if I leave you'll restart this IV. If you get a new bag of IV fluids, I'll return to my room like a good little boy. Don't you think it's better safe than sorry? I'd hate for you to lose your license by killing my friend when you've been warned that there is poison in that bag."

Fitz noticed hesitation in Beth's response. Without a word, she left the room and returned with a new bag of fluids. Fitz could tell she was angry as she hung the new bag and hooked it up to Katía's arm.

"Satisfied?" she asked.

"Thank you," he replied.

Katía held out her hand. "Thank you, Fitz. I'd be dead if it weren't for you."

He took her hand and gave it a squeeze. "No problem."

As Fitz turned to leave, he saw a Gainesville police officer he didn't know standing in the doorway.

With a puzzled expression, the officer said, "I'm Officer O'Conner. Are you Katía Bancroft?"

Officer O'Conner, a stout forty-two year old with short brown hair and brown eyes, eyed Fitz. "I need to speak with

Ms. Bancroft alone, please. Would everyone leave the room?"

Fitz realized he still held Katía's hand and released it. "Just tell him the truth," he said.

Back in his room, Beth said, "I suppose you are going to insist on a new bag of fluids, too."

"I'll live longer if you do that," Fitz replied.

Beth shook her head and left, returning a minute later with a new IV set up. "I'll have to poke you again," she said, readying everything to start the IV.

With the new fluids flowing, she took down the old bag, holding it upside down. When she reached the door, she noticed a drop fall from the bag. "Oh, my God! Security!"

CHAPTER 42

Fitz sat with Carlos, waiting for Katía to be released and trying to decide what to do next. He could tell that Officer O'Connor found it hard to believe that Crystal Samson could be involved in anything resembling what he had related.

The nurse's report confirming needle-sized holes in both IV bags had swayed him just a little. The nurse's insistence had helped to convince him to have the contents of the bags tested.

"I hope Ben thinks to come back for us," Carlos said.

"He'll be here. In fact, I'm surprised he's not already back."

The door opened, and Luna rolled Katía out into the waiting area.

"A few stitches and some IV fluids and I'm good as new," Katía said with a smile.

"And some pain medicine," Luna added as she helped Katía into a seat.

"How about you, Fitz?" Katía patted his knee. "You doing OK?"

"I'll make it."

"Sorry it took me so long," Ben said, walking in. "I can't believe you're already out."

"That police officer was quite the looker, but I don't think he believed a word I said about Crystal," Katía said, her speech a little slurred.

"Maybe finding out what is in those IV bags will convince them," Luna said.

"We need to go by a pharmacy and get Fitz's antibiotic and pain medicine prescriptions filled," Carlos stated, holding up the prescription.

"What a coincidence. I do, too," Katía added. "We're two peas in a pod."

"I usually use the Walgreens on Enota," Fitz said.

"I do, too," Katía replied. "Put it there." She held up a hand.

Fitz couldn't help laughing as he completed the high-five. "Let's get moving. I hope they're admitting Victor so we don't have to worry about him anymore."

"I wonder if he revealed who shot him. If he did, it might prompt the police to consider Crystal a suspect if she succeeds in her mission to do us in," Ben said.

Katía straightened in her chair. "She's not doing me in. I can take that woman."

"I believe you," Luna replied. "You're quite a character when you've had pain medicine."

With a laugh, they headed to the pharmacy.

* * * * *

Storming out of the hospital and spewing expletives, Crystal hopped into her Corvette and slammed the door. "I have to get rid of these people! They're going to ruin everything!" she ranted.

She had to concentrate to control the powerful car and avoid a speeding ticket as she drove back to the house. She tried to calm her rage and come up with a plan. As she tailgated the car in front of her, an idea emerged, prompting a grin like the Grinch's right after he had spoiled Christmas.

Using voice commands, she called Shannon and told her to meet her at the house. She pulled into the garage to swap the Corvette for her BMW X5.

Starting to get into the car, she asked Shannon, "Victor uses zip-ties to bind people's wrists. Do you know how he does that?"

"No, I don't know how he does that," Shannon barked.

Crystal went rummaging through a cabinet in the garage till she found a bag of the ties. "We'll have to figure it out as we go. We have to hurry back to the hospital and follow them when they leave," she explained.

"I take it the potassium didn't work then," Shannon replied.

"No. The old fool figured out what I was doing and ripped out his IV. I hope it got the woman. That would be one down."

"What about Victor?"

"He said they are taking him to surgery, so he's out of commission. It's up to us now."

They rode in silence till Shannon said, "I'm not sure I can kill anyone."

"You're just going to have to suck it up and do it. You realize if word gets out, we'll both go to prison."

Shannon didn't respond, so Crystal kept talking. "We'll lose everything we've worked so hard for. You won't be able to buy the nice baubles you're used to."

Crystal glanced over and thought she saw Shannon roll her eyes. "You surely don't think we'd make the money we do just from the cleaning business. That's pocket change compared to what the opioids bring in."

Shannon remained silent for a couple of minutes, then said, "If we do this, you're going to have to share more of the wealth."

Rage flooded Crystal's spirit. "Are you blackmailing me?"

"No. I'm just saying that if I'm out here killing people for you, I think I deserve a large raise. That was supposed to be Victor's thing."

"If you want a raise, you'll have to figure out how to bring in more money. I need everything I get right now."

Crystal pulled into the hospital parking lot and parked so she could see the emergency room doors. Tense silence pressed down when she turned off the vehicle.

"I hope one of them leaves in a hearse," Crystal said, trying to break the tension.

Shannon didn't reply, and the silence continued to press on Crystal's nerves. It was then she noticed the police cars parked along the way to the ER drop-off. *What if they called the police and told them about me? If they're dead, they can't testify. I have to make sure that happens.*

Finally, an Outback pulled up to the doors.

"Isn't that one of their vehicles?" Crystal asked.

"I think so."

Crystal cranked the BMW and watched. Five of them loaded into the Outback.

"It looks like they stopped her IV in time." Crystal ended the sentence with a string of profanity.

As the Outback pulled out, she backed out of the parking place and followed.

CHAPTER 43

The last light of day seeped away as they left the pharmacy with their medication in hand. On the drive back to Kroger, a soft rain began to fall. Katía was still goofy from the pain medicine.

"I love rain. It'll be nice to watch it roll down the windows. It sounds so nice, too," Katía said.

Stress squeezed Fitz's heart. "We need to get you somewhere you can lie down and be comfortable."

"I'm fine as frog hair," Katía replied, patting his leg.

"You might not feel so fine when the pain medicine wears off," Luna suggested.

"No problem. They gave me a whole bottle full." She shook the pill bottle.

"We need a new plan," Fitz said. "We still haven't found the stash of pills."

"I think we should let the police take it from here," Luna said.

"Yeah. They already know who's involved and what they have done," Carlos agreed. "All three should be arrested before morning."

"That's true only if Officer O'Conner believes our stories. He seemed to have reservations," Fitz noted.

"Two of us gave him the same story," Katía said. "Where two or more are gathered… they ought to be believed. The folks at church aren't going to believe all of this."

"If Victor is an enforcer for the Cañería Cartel, they probably have reinforcements on the way," Ben stated. "Our best move is to stay hidden. You did mention the cartel to the police, right?"

"I did. He said he's not aware of any activity by that cartel in the area," Fitz replied.

"Great. So he didn't believe you," Ben said.

"I don't think so. Crystal called Victor a loyal puppy, so maybe Zee was right about his lying," Fitz added.

Ben turned left onto Limestone Parkway, then took an immediate right into the Kroger complex.

"Oooh, McDonald's looks good," Katía said as they passed by it.

"We will need supper," Ben added. "I'll get everyone's order and come back."

He backed in next to Zee's car on the far left side of the lot. The others gathered around the Outback to check on the injured ones.

"Are you OK?" Victoria asked as Fitz climbed out. She reached to hug him, but he held up his hand.

"Sore ribs," he said. "Yeah, we're OK, especially Katía."

"Oh, look! All of my friends are here! How special," Katía said as she stood up from the seat. "Who wants McDonald's for supper? Wait, it's drizzling. I'm getting back in the car."

The lights of a car parking two lanes over lit them up for a moment, then went out.

"That's a good idea," Fitz said, holding the door open for her.

*　*　*　*　*

Crystal was three cars behind the Outback in the left turn lane leading to Limestone Parkway.

"I bet they're hiding in the Kroger parking lot this time," she said.

Shannon didn't reply. *I wonder if I'm going to be able to count on her.*

The light changed, and two of the three cars followed suit, turning into the Kroger complex and keeping distance between her and the Outback. Crystal slowed to let them get ahead then crept along, turning two lanes over from where the Outback went.

She stopped for a minute and observed where it parked before selecting her parking place. There was a whole crowd gathered around the Outback once they got out.

"How many of them are there?" Crystal gasped.

"I think I see ten. That's too many. There's no way we can do this," Shannon stated.

"We have to do this, Shannon. There is no other option."

"Why don't we just go get rid of the drugs and claim it was all Victor's doing?"

"Because there are two IV bags with my handiwork in them. We either get rid of the witnesses, or we go to prison. Which do you prefer?"

Shannon shrank in the seat and went silent.

"That's what I thought," Crystal said. "We have to figure out how to take out all of these people at once."

"Without an assault rifle, I don't see that happening," Shannon replied.

"Do you know how to shoot one of those?"

"I have no idea. I guess you put bullets in and pull the trigger like any other gun. That would make a big scene, and we're likely to get caught. Someone will notice us driving off," Shannon said.

"Yeah, there are too many people here. I think Victor keeps an assault rifle at his house." Crystal pushed her hair behind her ears. She asked, more to herself than to Shannon, "Should we go get it or try to surprise them with the two guns we have?"

"Are you an idiot? If we try to take them now, we'd have to haul them out of here in front of all these people. We should come back with the assault rifle after the store closes," Shannon suggested, wringing her hands. "But you have to shoot it."

Crystal glared at Shannon, then decided she was probably right. *I hate to wait but with the parking lot empty, I could mow them down and take off.*

She started backing out, then had second thoughts. "What if they leave while we're gone?" She pulled back into the parking space.

"Why would they leave? As far as they know they're safe and sound."

"If I were them, I wouldn't stay in one place very long," Crystal replied.

"So you want to just walk up and say, 'Would you all please come with us so we can kill you?'"

"We do have two guns, you know."

"They have guns, too. Remember the hole in my car?" Shannon snipped.

Crystal stopped and tried to think of options. A cold smile grew on her face as one option came to mind.

"I need to make a phone call," she said. About to open her phone, she realized it would light up her face. "But not here. They might see me."

She drove across the parking lot and parked facing away from her quarry.

"Hey, Frank. This is Crystal Samson. How are you? … The truth is I'm a little frazzled right now. Victor Pelfrey has been shot. … I heard you responded to the call that put him in the hospital. … Let me tell you what really happened. The other two people you talked two plus a few more have been picketing my business and harassing my workers. They claim I'm running a sweat shop and treating the workers badly. Anyway, Victor went out to run them off, and they started shooting. I'm afraid he returned fire and hit the woman. …"

She winked at Shannon. "I don't know how to explain the man's injuries unless they were self-inflicted to try to make it look worse. He was the one doing the shooting. His name is Joe Fitzgerald, and he seems off his rocker. … Victor was pretty goofy when I stopped by. It must have been pain medicine. There is no telling what he told you. … Now that's inventive. I can't believe they would lie and tell you I tried to poison them. I did step into their rooms and tell them to stay off my property. … Thanks for believing me. I think that man and woman are the ones who need to be prosecuted. … Thanks. I hope he's going to be OK, too. It was good talking to you. Bye."

"That was quite the tale," Shannon said after Crystal disconnected.

"He bought it and said he was just going to let analyzing the contents of the IV bags slide under the rug. He is going to question Victor again, so we have to get to him and get our stories straight before Frank gets back."

"Good. We're off the hook, so let's just go home."

"No, Shannon. We still have to eliminate these people… right after we talk to Victor."

CHAPTER 44

Ben and Zee returned from McDonald's with ten sets of Quarter Pounders, fries, and drinks. Snickers and King sniffed eagerly from the back seat. Fitz, Luna and Carlos pulled in right after Ben, having been to Sparkles to retrieve Fitz's car and, more importantly, Buffett.

Ben and Zee distributed the meals to everyone where they were huddled in their cars against the chill rain.

"Do you want to join us? We can put the dogs in the back," Ben asked.

"No, thanks. I'm going to spend some time with Buffett," Fitz replied, running his hand down Buffett's back, who was snuggled in his lap. Buffett stood as soon as he smelled hamburger. While Carlos drove Fitz's car back, Buffett had been all over Fitz, sniffing and rubbing. Fitz believed the cat knew he had been injured.

"OK, but we probably need to talk after supper," Ben said.

"You're right. Is Katía OK?"

"Yeah. She's coming down from her pain med high. Luna and Carlos are in the car with her."

"Good. I'll join you in a bit." He got out, moved to the driver's seat, then tore a chunk of meat from his hamburger for Buffett. "We're in a real mess, buddy. I can't figure out how we're going to get out of it, either."

"Meow."

"I'm glad you're confident. … Maybe I should just try to figure out our next move instead of the whole problem. One step at a time."

"Meow."

Fitz thought while he wolfed down his meal. "I didn't realize I was that hungry."

"Meow." Buffett rubbed his chin.

"Sorry. I ate it all."

Buffett hopped to the back seat, and Fitz heard him lapping water.

"We're really off our routine. I need to get your litter emptied. How's the food level?"

"Meow."

Fitz pulled the hood of his coat up against the rain, retrieved a Berretta and ammo from the lock box, scooped the litter, and refilled Buffett's food and water.

"You really are an extraordinary cat, you know. You're willing to live in this little space and put up with the likes of me."

Buffett nudged Fitz's hand with his nose, and Fitz complied with an ear scratch.

"I need to go talk to Ben and Zee. I won't be gone long this time."

"Meow."

Fitz slid into the back seat of Ben's Outback to a flurry of noses and licks.

"Snickers, in the back," Ben commanded, and Snickers obeyed. King joined her, needing a little boost to get over the seat back.

"That was easy," Ben said.

"We hang with smart dogs," Zee noted.

"I think we have a big problem," Fitz said, steering the discussion to their predicament.

"It's not that big," Ben replied. "We just have to stay alive until the police analyze the contents of the IV bags and put Crystal and Shannon in jail."

"If Victor was telling the truth, we have the firepower of a drug cartel after us," Fitz added.

"How long do you think it will take for them to be arrested," Zee asked.

"It all depends on how backed up the lab is. It could take several days," Fitz replied.

"Oh. I was hoping they were already working on it," Ben said. "It's hard to hide this many people in one spot. We sort of stick out. Should we split up?"

"Splitting up makes us less conspicuous but deletes our fire power if we're found. I'm leaning toward staying together so we have more guns if we're attacked," Fitz answered.

"How many more guns do you have?" Ben asked.

"I only have two left."

They sat in silence for a moment, rain making a soothing sound on the top of the car. Fitz tried to think the issue through logically, but his gut kept telling him they needed to move. He gave up and went with his intuition.

"Something is telling me we need to move. We're going to be too obvious once the store closes."

"That's true. Won't be anybody but us here then," Zee said.

"We need a place that's open twenty-four hours a day," Fitz added.

"The only places I know of that are open all night are Waffle House and Huddle House. Their parking lots are so small that we'd be sitting ducks," Ben observed.

"The hospital's always open," Zee said.

"Do you think they'd guess we might go back there?" Ben asked.

"How about the Braselton hospital?" Fitz added.

"That's a great idea. It's far enough away it shouldn't even cross their minds," Ben replied.

"It crossed my mind," Fitz said.

"True, but it's better than being the only cars in the parking lot," Ben said. "The police will probably run us off anyway."

"I cain't think of a better idea," Zee added.

Fitz's mind was at war with itself. *If we park in the ER lot, we are exposing others to danger if they find us. If we don't hide where there are other people around, we are putting ourselves at greater risk of being found. They're both no win situations.*

He realized his finger nails were digging into his palms and relaxed his hands.

"Fitz? Oh, Fitz, come in please," came from the front seat.

"Yeah?" Fitz answered.

"I was saying let's go ahead and use the facilities here, stock up on some snacks, and take off. The parking lot is already starting to thin out," Ben said.

"I agree. It's time to go."

They got out and spread the plan to the others. The whole crew hit the store and returned with plenty of snacks and drinks for the night.

Ben led the caravan to the Braselton hospital. Luna drove Katía's car. Since Victoria didn't drive, María agreed to drive Fitz's car, even though she didn't have a license.

On the drive down, the dream about Sharon returned to Fitz's thoughts. *What did you mean it would be OK? It's not OK. The only thing that's OK is I don't care whether I live or die. It won't matter if they find me and gun me down. I do care about these other people, so I have to try to keep them safe. One already got shot in the arm and nearly bled out. I'm really worried about her.*

Fitz felt Sharon so close that he looked around, half expecting to see her. *I still miss you, you know. That's not OK either.*

"I know it hurts, but you need to let me go and live your life. It's OK," emerged from the void into his mind. He looked around again, even turning to check the back seat, which drew a groan of pain.

"What is wrong? Did you lose something?" María asked.

"No. I was just looking…" He stopped himself before telling her he was looking for Sharon.

Ben located a spot in the ER lot with enough room for all six cars to park next to each other. The rain had stopped, and the air was crisp and damp.

The clock on Fitz's dashboard read 11:14pm when María cut the ignition switch. He got out, started to stretch, but cut it short with a wince from the pain in his ribs. He walked to Katía's car, where Luna emerged from the driver's seat.

"How is she?" Fitz asked.

"I think she's better. She kept saying she could have driven so that I could ride with Carlos," Luna answered.

Fitz poked his head in through the driver's door. "Hey. How ya doing?"

"I'm OK. It still hurts, but it's nothing I can't live with. How about you?"

"I was doing good till I tried to stretch."

"Yeah, that's not good on the ribs," she replied.

"I'm going to check on the others," Fitz said, then walked to Alejandro and Victoria's car.

"You folks doing OK?" he asked.

"I'm getting tired of living out of the car, but other than that, we're fine," Victoria answered. "I hope this is over soon."

"Me, too," Fitz replied.

Fitz walked back to where Ben and Zee were leaning against Zee's car.

"I think we should set up watches so the others can get some sleep," Ben said.

"Spoken like a true Army Ranger," Fitz replied.

"You were an Army Ranger?" Zee asked.

"You sound like you find that hard to believe," Ben chuckled.

"I would've never guessed," Zee replied.

"You should stop before you dig your hole too deep," Fitz chuckled.

Ben said, "The mice have hidden. Now we wait for the cat to make her move."

CHAPTER 45

Crystal's hands trembled as she locked the BMW to go into the hospital. She wasn't sure whether the cause was anxiety or rage. Upon reaching the front door, she noticed a sign stating that the doors were locked and that she would have to enter through the emergency room.

That discovery prompted a string of loud curses followed by Shannon's shushing her. Cystal balled both fists as she reined in her mouth.

"He'd better be out of recovery," She grumped as they started the long walk to the emergency room entrance. "Who closes their doors by nine o'clock? That's just ridiculous!"

She stomped down the sidewalk, had second thoughts, then led Shannon to the car.

"I don't want to have to make this walk twice. Let's park closer to the ER."

When they finally got inside the hospital, the volunteer, a seventy-something lady who was elegantly dressed, told them that Victor was still in recovery.

"Could you call and ask how much longer they think he'll be?" Crystal asked, forcing sweetness into her tone.

After making the call, the lady said, "Their best guess is within the hour. One can never give a precise time on getting out of recovery, though. I'll be happy to direct you to the post-surgery waiting room."

Crystal's fist clenched beneath the counter. She couldn't afford the delay, but she couldn't let Frank get to Victor before she did, either. Realizing she had hesitated to respond, she said, "That would be great. Where is it?"

With directions in hand, Crystal led Shannon down the hall far enough not to be overheard, then whispered, "We have to split up. You wait on Victor, and I'll go to his house to get the assault rifle."

"You know where he lives? How will you get in?"

"I have a key."

"You have a key?" Shannon said, baffled.

"Don't ask. Do you have the story straight?"

"Yeah."

"Ok, tell it to me."

"They were protesting at Sparkles and harassing the workers. Victor went out to run them off. They fired on him, and he returned fire, hitting the woman. He was hit twice. The old man inflicted injuries on himself and made up the torture story. Sound about right?"

"Perfect. I love your attention to detail."

Crystal left Shannon to find the waiting room and returned to her car. She made the drive to Victor's house, let herself in, and headed to the gun cabinet. Unlocking the door, she spied the assault rifle. She trusted that the magazines next to the rifle were the correct ammo. She grabbed all four magazines. *It was nice of him to have these already loaded.*

Starting to close the case, she decided to take a deer rifle, too. *Just in case.* She started to check her watch, but her hands were too full. *I'll see the time in the car.*

She pushed the start button and pulled out her phone. The clock read 10:15. *Forty-five minutes till Kroger closes.* The pressure of time restarted the trembling. She had to brace her hands on the steering wheel to text Shannon asking if Victor was out of recovery.

"Not yet."

"On my way back," she replied. *Actually, we don't have to be at Kroger right at eleven. It's probably better to be a few minutes late… let the parking lot clear more.* She relaxed into the luxurious seat and drove back to the hospital.

After parking, she brushed her hair and spruced up her makeup. *I need all my weapons to sell this story if Frank shows up.*

Shannon was sitting alone, scrolling on her phone, when Crystal entered the waiting room. Before she sat down, the woman at the desk called, "Family for Victor Pelfrey." She informed them he was out of recovery and gave them his room number.

"I hope he's not so sedated that he can't remember the story we're about to give him," Crystal said just before pushing open the door to Victor's room. She paused with her hand on the door. "Don't mention the assault rifle," she whispered.

Victor's eyes were closed when they entered. Crystal said softly, "Hey, Victor. How are you feeling?"

He grunted, but that was all. Crystal walked over and patted his forearm. His eyes popped open, and he started to sit up, as if to flee.

"It's OK. It's just us," Crystal said, gently pushing him back down.

"I thought someone was after me. They had a gun. I guess I was dreaming."

"You're in the hospital and just got out of surgery. They removed the bullets and said you'll be OK in a few weeks," Shannon said, stepping around to the opposite side of the bed.

"I see." He relaxed his head into the pillow. "I tried to take care of them, but they shot me twice. I couldn't keep going."

"It's OK, Victor. I appreciate all you did. Are you alert?"

His eyes closed, and he didn't answer. Crystal reached to tap his shoulder, stopping when she realized that was the one that had been shot. She redirected her hand to his forearm and shook.

"Victor, I need you to wake up."

"Do we have a sleepy patient?" a male voice called from the door.

Looking up, Crystal watched Frank enter the room.

"Yeah, he's sleepy. The nurse told us to try to rouse him here and there," Crystal said, forcing a smile.

"I had them call when he was out of surgery. I was hoping to get his statement."

"Have you arrested those creeps yet? I can't believe they did this to Victor," Crystal said, ramping up the concern.

"Actually, we can't issue the arrest warrant until I have his confirmation of the incident. Otherwise, it's just your word against that other guy's."

"We haven't gotten him awake but once," Crystal said, "And that time he thought someone was chasing him with a gun."

"He even tried to get out of the bed," Shannon added.

"I see," Frank said, rubbing his chin. "It looks like I made a wasted trip. I'll have to come back later."

"What about Shannon?" Crystal asked.

"What do you mean?" Frank asked.

"She knows what happened. You could take her statement."

Crystal cringed when that came out of her mouth. *I have to walk that back. I can't have the police looking for them while I'm after them, too.*

"Wait, never mind. She only knows what happened because I told her. She was out of the office when they attacked."

"I see. That would be considered hearsay and wouldn't hold up. I'll check back on Victor later in the night. Maybe he'll be more alert."

"Thanks," Crystal said as Frank turned to leave.

"You are quite welcome," he replied.

"Whew," Crystal sighed after Frank was gone. "I almost screwed up."

"If you had let me give a statement, they would have arrested them and we would be done with this mess," Shannon said.

"They could still tell the police about our drug thing. We can't rest till they're dead."

Crystal checked her watch. 10:49. "The store's about to close. Let's give Victor another thirty minutes to wake up, then we have to go."

Shannon sat down, and Crystal paced. Every five minutes, she would shake his forearm to see if he would come to. On the fifth try, his eyes stayed open and he seemed to understand what they were talking about.

Crystal talked him through the story they had developed and had him repeat it back to her. She went over it three times before he got it right.

"I need you to keep repeating that to yourself over and over. When Frank comes back, I want you to tell him exactly what we've rehearsed. OK?"

"Got it," Victor said.

Crystal and Shannon returned to the BMW.

"You drive, and I'll do the rifle," Crystal directed.

They took their seats, and Crystal reached behind the driver's seat, pulling the assault rifle off the floor.

"What are you doing?" Shannon asked, her voice laced with terror. "Somebody could see that."

"I have to load it."

"Not here."

"Where would you suggest then?" She reached back for one of the magazines.

"In a place that's less… peoply," Shannon replied.

"I don't think there is a place between here and the shopping center."

"At least let me move to a less crowded part of the parking lot."

"OK. Go," Crystal said.

Shannon drove to the far corner of the outpatient parking lot. There were no cars nearby and no one was walking around.

Crystal studied the rifle, then reached up and flicked on the cabin light.

"What are you doing?" Shannon whispered.

"I have to figure this thing out, and I can't do it in the dark."

Shannon turned her head continuously, looking for anyone who might see them.

She grabbed Crystal's arm and squeezed hard. "A car is coming! It's coming this way!"

Crystal jammed the assault rifle and magazine onto the back floorboard and whipped out her phone. The car pulled up beside them and signaled for Shannon to roll down her window. It was hospital security.

"Hey, ma'am. Do you ladies need help?" the security guard asked.

"No, sir," Crystal called across Shannon. "We were leaving when I realized I needed to text my sister and tell her my brother came through his surgery OK. We pulled over here to be out of the way because I can't text with the car moving."

"I'm glad to hear he came through OK. Take care," he said and drove off.

Crystal pulled the rifle back out, figured out how to get the magazine attached, located the safety, and they took off.

As they approached the Kroger lot, Crystal could see that Shannon had a death grip on the steering wheel. Crystal's nails were digging into her palms.

"Remember the plan. You're going to pull in front of them so that they are on my side. Keep circling till we're sure they are all taken care of, then we get out to make sure."

"Got it," Shannon said, her voice hoarse.

Shannon pulled into the lot and turned toward their quarry. No cars were there. Crystal took her finger off the window power button, and her mouth dropped open. "What the… Where did they go?" She thought she heard Shannon breathe a sigh of relief.

CHAPTER 46

Crystal scanned the parking lot, not believing her eyes. Shannon had stopped right in the middle.

"Maybe they're at McDonald's," Crystal said. "Drive through there."

Shannon obliged and drove around the fast food place. They weren't there, either.

"Pull into that last spot. We have to figure out where they went."

With the car stopped, Crystal reached into the back seat and retrieved the laptop. Handing it to Shannon, she said, "See if any of their phones are powered up."

"Hide the gun!" Shannon croaked.

Crystal thought out loud while Shannon opened the cellular connection to check. "They seem to like parking lots. I would want a place where restrooms are available, so it would need to be open twenty-four hours."

She paused, searching her mind for places that were open all night.

"Noooo… They couldn't have been at the hospital! Do you think?"

Shannon replied, "It would be risky going back there. They should have known we might be checking on Victor. None of their phones are showing up."

"If I were hiding from me, I'd go back to the hospital. Let's go check it out," Crystal directed.

"Surely you're not going to open fire at the hospital. That would be a guaranteed prison term."

"We can't do anything till we find them. Let's go."

Crystal pulled the rifle back out as Shannon drove through the various lots at the hospital, but they didn't see the cars of their prey. She pulled into a parking place in the last lot they searched.

"Now what?" Shannon asked.

"I can't believe they weren't here. I felt so sure of it. What are some other options?"

"Crystal, this is like looking for a needle in a haystack. Gainesville's a big town, and they could be anywhere."

"Do you want to just give up and go turn ourselves in to the police?"

Shannon didn't reply.

"I didn't think so. Finding them is not optional. We have to, or we're finished. What about the hospital down in Braselton? Do you think they went there?"

Shannon paused before answering. "That does make sense. It's a long way off, and they might think we wouldn't look there."

"Let's go."

"If they're not there, we'll have wasted a whole hour. It's a thirty minute drive just to get there."

"I don't care. I have a hunch this is right. Let's get moving."

"You had a hunch they were here," Shannon growled.

She exited the hospital parking lot, worked her way through town, and took I-985 south toward the Braselton campus. As they approached the turn into the hospital, Crystal switched off the safety for the assault rifle.

"Are you crazy? Put that away," Shannon barked.

"I want to be ready just in case we need it. What if they fire on us?"

*   *   *   *   *

Ben and Zee walked back after taking Snickers and King for a walk in the grass. Fitz was still leaning against Zee's car. He checked his watch, and it read 12:33am. He yawned as they approached.

"I had a good idea while we were walking the dogs," Ben said. "We could just go to the police office and wait. We should be safe there."

Fitz replied, "That's a good idea, but they won't let us hang out there."

"Not even if we tell them a deranged woman is after us? We could request protection," Ben replied.

"They'd probably think we're crazy and lock us up," Zee said.

Fitz added, "Zee's right, but I think they would just run us off instead of locking us up. There would only be a couple of officers there. Most of them will be out on patrol, so they wouldn't want to babysit this crew."

"How about the jail?" Ben asked.

Fitz laughed. "They wouldn't even let us in at this time of night."

"I'm afraid that woman might try something crazy, like come at us with assault rifles," Ben continued.

"I don't think... Uh-oh."

"What?" Ben asked. He followed Fitz's eyes to the hospital security vehicle making its way through the parking lots. "Uh-oh is right."

"They won't let us stay here," Fitz said.

"We can buy a bit more time by walking into the ER," Zee suggested.

"Spoken like the voice of experience," Ben replied.

Zee just grinned.

"Let's get the others moving toward the ER," Fitz directed.

"We can say we're bringing Katía back with an infection," Zee added.

"You are a resourceful guy, aren't you?" Ben chuckled.

They got everyone out of the cars and were headed to the ER entrance by the time the patrol car arrived. Ben took Katía's good arm like he was assisting her to walk. The security guard waved as he passed by.

The car stopped, backed up, and the guard rolled the window down.

"I just want to let you know that they'll only let one person back with the patient. If the waiting room gets too full, we'll need some of you to wait outside," the guard said.

"Thank you. We'll do that. We're just concerned about her," Fitz replied.

As they walked through the door, a woman at the desk asked, "May I help you?" Her eyes narrowed as people kept entering.

Zee stepped forward and said, "We're waiting on someone who's already back and being seen."

"I might have to ask some of you to leave if we get busy. We don't normally allow this many visitors, but it's a slow night."

"Thanks," Zee replied.

They found an area with enough seats to accommodate everyone.

Fitz bought a coffee out of the vending machine. Taking a sip he said, "It's not as good as what I make, but it'll do for this time of night."

"We need to find a place where we can get some sleep," Ben said.

"Yeah, this isn't going to be it," Fitz answered. "Zee, you have your phone with you?"

"Yep. It's charged and ready."

"Pull up the map and let's see what else we can find around here," Fitz directed.

"Tell me again why we don't just check into a hotel?" Ben asked.

"Because she might have friends on the police force checking for credit card transactions," Fitz said.

"At this point, I'd be willing to bet not. Besides, she'd have to break our doors down to get in."

"Ain't no way I can afford a hotel," Zee said.

"You two can stay with me. I'll cover it," Ben said. "See if you can find one nearby."

Zee pecked at the phone with his finger. "It looks like there's one by I-985."

"Perfect. I say we go there," Ben said.

Fitz stewed, warring with the lure of a shower versus the fear of being found.

Katía returned from the restroom. "I'm so tired. I think I'm going to curl up on a couple of these seats."

Fitz scanned the weary faces of his group, and he was swayed. "OK, let's try a hotel."

The eyes around him brightened. "I can't wait to go to sleep," Sofía said with a yawn.

"Could I see your phone?" Ben asked.

Zee passed it over, and he studied the map. "We turn right out of the hospital and go straight. The hotel is just past I-985. It shouldn't be hard to stay together this time of night. Let's go."

The crew returned to their cars and cranked them, with Fitz insisting he would drive this time. They followed Ben toward the road. Fitz brought up the rear. While they were waiting for the light to change at the end of the parking lot, he noticed a BMW turn in.

CHAPTER 47

Shannon huffed as she slowed to make the turn into the hospital. Crystal had her eyes scrunched trying to make out the cars in the parking lot up ahead. She jerked her head around looking behind her.

"That's them! It has to be! Yes! That's the old guy's Highlander in the back. Hurry! Loop around and head back out!"

Crystal's grip tensed on the assault rifle. Her heart started pounding in response to a rush of adrenaline. "We've finally got them," she growled.

Crystal watched as Shannon drove. "They're turning right," she said as the line of cars began to move.

Shannon made the loop and headed toward the exit. As she approached, the light changed back to red. She put her foot on the brake, and Crystal screamed, "Don't stop! Nothing's coming! Go!"

Shannon blasted through the light, turning right onto the four-laned Friendship Road. The line of taillights was just ahead.

"This is perfect. There's no one around. Pass them and I'll take them out one car at a time. Hurry!"

Shannon accelerated, and Crystal rolled down the window. As they pulled up beside the Highlander, Crystal leaned out the window and pulled the trigger. Three rounds fired, and the kickback knocked her back into the car. The bullets went over the vehicle.

"I wasn't expecting that," she said, repositioning her grip. "This thing's powerful."

Shannon had slowed down.

"Catch back up to them. I'm ready this time," Crystal ordered.

Shannon hit the gas. As she was about to pass the Highlander, it whipped over in front of her. She hit the brakes just enough to avoid hitting it.

"Stay on his tail," Crystal shouted.

Shannon sped up, getting right on the Highlander's tail. Crystal folded her right leg, put her knee on the seat, and pushed her upper body out the window. She leveled the rifle at the car and took aim toward the driver's seat.

The Highlander's taillights flashed, and Shannon slammed on the brakes just as Crystal began to fire. The jolt was so sudden, it threw Crystal forward, and she dropped the rifle. She grasped at the door with her left hand. Her fingers slid along the roof fabric till her nails dug into the molding. The nails bent under the force, and Crystal toppled out of the car.

She hit the road at fifteen miles an hour, rolling over and over.

Shannon whipped the BMW to the left, away from where Crystal had fallen. When she came to a complete stop, she jumped out, having forgotten to shift the vehicle into park. It started rolling forward. Shannon caught up, jumped back in, and slammed it into park.

She ran around the car, hands to her mouth. She saw Crystal writhing on the road and burst into tears.

"Oh, no! Are you OK?"

"Ooooh," Crystal moaned, pain wracking her whole body. "No! I'm not OK, you idiot! Everything hurts!"

"At least you're alive. I was afraid you'd be dead."

Crystal rolled onto her back and moved her arms and legs. "I don't think I broke anything. Where's the rifle? Find the rifle!"

Shannon scanned the area and noticed a gleam off the side of the road a few feet back. Moving closer, she picked up the rifle.

"Found it. I don't think we'll be using this anymore," she said, noting the broken stock and slight bend to the barrel.

"Help me up," Crystal ordered.

Back on her feet, she checked her hair. Blood oozed from the back of her head. Elbows, knees, and one hand oozed from road rash.

"We need to get you to the hospital," Shannon said.

"And just how are we going to explain this?" Crystal barked.

Blue lights flashed, and a patrol car stopped on the other side of the road.

"Hide that!"

Shannon rushed to toss the rifle through the open passenger window. Crystal tried to come up with what to say.

The officer crossed the median but kept her distance. "Is there a problem, ladies?"

"Yeah. This crazy drunk nearly ran us off the road. He stopped, and I got out yelling at him. The next thing I know, he put the car in reverse, and I tried to run. I tripped and splatted on the asphalt. He took off and disappeared," Crystal said.

"Do I need to call an ambulance for you?" the officer asked.

"I don't think so. Nothing seems to be broken."

"Did either of you get the tag number of the vehicle?"

"No, but it was an older Highlander. It happened so fast, I'm not even sure what color it was," Shannon answered.

"Have you been drinking?" the officer asked.

"We certainly have not," Shannon answered, hands on her hips and standing on one foot for emphasis.

"All right, you can put your foot down. You folks need to move on. I'll report the vehicle, and I hope the rest of your night goes better."

The officer returned to her patrol car.

"Let's go," Crystal said, gingerly sitting down in the passenger seat. "Hurry! We have to catch up to them." She pulled the deer rifle from the back seat and proceeded to load it.

"Enough, Crystal," Shannon screeched. "It's time to go home and let the process play out. The police have believed you so far. We will say they are lying, and they'll continue to believe us. Put the rifle back."

"No. I'm going to take an oxy, then we're going to finish this. I can't take any chances."

She fished the medication out of her purse and swallowed a pill. "Come on! Let's go."

"I'm driving us home."

Crystal replaced the medication bottle and pulled out her pistol. "It's not optional, Shannon. We're going after these people."

Shannon glanced at the gun leveled at her heart. "So you're going to kill me, too?"

"Not unless you refuse to do as I'm telling you. Now catch up to them."

* * * * *

After hitting the brakes, Fitz gunned the gas. He watched in the rearview mirror and thought he saw something fall out of the BMW. *I hope that was Crystal.*

The BMW fell behind as Fitz surged forward. *It looks like I dodged a bullet.* He chuckled at his thought, then tried to relax his grip on the steering wheel.

"You OK, Buffett?"

Buffett jumped out of the back seat and climbed into Fitz's lap.

"I don't think she has been arrested yet," he explained to the cat. Buffett purred as he got comfortable. A jolt of panic hit when Fitz realized that Crystal and Shannon could get back into the car and keep coming.

He zoomed ahead, catching up with Ben at the head of the line of cars. Rolling down his window, he signaled for Ben to do the same.

He yelled, "She found us and tried to shoot me with an assault rifle. Go to the Jameson Inn on Thurmond Tanner. You'll have to turn right on Spout Springs. Maybe that will throw her off track. And hurry!"

"Got it," Ben called back.

Fitz slowed and dropped back to the end of the line. *I'd rather it be me than one of the others if she catches up.* He kept an eye on his rearview mirror as he let the others get ahead out of sight.

Approaching the light at Spout Springs Road, an idea struck. Fitz hit the brakes and whipped right into a parking lot just before the intersection. Cutting the lights, he grabbed the Beretta and jumped out.

He waited less than a minute before seeing lights approaching. *I hope they slow down trying to decide which way to go.*

He was right. The vehicle slowed. It was definitely a BMW like the one from which they had fired on him. He waited, searching the windows to make sure he was shooting at the right vehicle. In the dim light from the street lights, he caught Crystal's eye.

As he leveled his pistol to fire, the passenger window rolled down. He focused, fired, and the front tire went flat. Then he noticed the rifle sticking out the window.

Running as fast as his old legs would move, he hurried to get to his car. A shot fired, and a bullet ricocheted off the sidewalk about ten feet away.

He dared to look back and saw the BMW coming to a stop. As he jumped into the driver's seat, another shot hit the back door.

Fitz gunned the car, careened around the corner, and headed for the exit onto Spout Springs Road. Another shot cracked, but the bullet missed. As he turned onto the road, he heard Crystal screaming, "Hurry! He's getting away!"

Fitz was torn between stopping to check on Buffett and getting away till he felt the cat nudge his elbow.

"You're still OK!" he said as Buffett climbed into his lap. Stroking his fur, he said, "I think your catness is wearing off on me. It appears I've gained some extra lives."

CHAPTER 48

Fitz caught up with the others at a traffic light. He followed them to the Jameson Inn, sure Crystal and Shannon wouldn't be getting that flat fixed anytime soon.

He hurried over and opened the door to Katía's Prius. She had insisted on driving, too.

"I didn't want you to have to push the door with your left arm."

"Thanks, but I could have pushed it with my leg. How are you feeling?"

"Better. As long as I don't move the wrong way it's not too bad."

"Did you take any pain medicine?"

"No, recovering alcoholics need to avoid that kind of stuff," Fitz replied, rubbing the back of his neck.

Katía wiggled around, protecting her left shoulder. Fitz offered his hand and helped her out of her seat.

"I'm taking another pill as soon as I can. I hope it will help me get some sleep," she said.

They followed the others into the lobby. Fitz overheard Ben requesting four rooms. Pulling out his wallet, he checked to see if he had enough to help pay. *I can do sixty. I need to keep the rest just in case.*

He pulled out the money and offered it to Ben when he came over with the keys.

"Keep your money. This is coming out of my emergency fund," Ben said. He handed one key to Alejandro, one to Carlos, and one to Katía. "I was planning on you and María sharing."

"Perfect," Katía replied.

They located their rooms, and Ben asked, "What happened with the loony toon?"

"I managed to shoot out one of her tires. It'll be awhile before she's back in action," Fitz answered.

Everyone said good night as the entered their rooms.

Closing the door to the hotel room, Zee said, "Look at the paintings over the beds. I think I know that artist." He walked over and studied the signature. "Yep, it's him. He's a famous Gainesville artist. I wondered through their studios a few times before I got my car. Nice folks. They didn't seem to mind me being there."

"Any ideas for our next move?" Ben asked.

"I vote for sleep," Zee said. "I'll take the sofa."

"I meant for getting Crystal behind bars," Ben replied.

"Could I borrow your phone, Zee? I'll check and see if the arrest warrant has been issued yet. If so, I'll tell them where they can find her."

He dialed the sheriff's office. "I hope Geraldine's on. … Hey, is Geraldine on tonight? … Could I speak to her? … Hey, Geraldine. It's Fitz."

"What kind of trouble are you in now?" she asked.

"What makes you think I'm in trouble?"

"Why else would you be calling me?"

"I see. Well, you're sort of right. I'm calling to see if an arrest warrant has been issued for Crystal Samson."

He whispered to Ben and Zee, "She's looking it up."

"I'm not seeing one for her but let me dig a little deeper. Uh-oh. I do see a warrant for your arrest," she said.

Fitz's eyes went wide. "You have to be kidding. There's a warrant for my arrest? What for?"

"It says it's for the attempted murder of Victor Pelfrey."

"Attempted murder of Victor Pelfrey?" Fitz repeated, not believing his ears.

"Do you mind telling me where you are?" Geraldine asked.

"No, I don't care to tell you where I am right now. Thanks, Geraldine." Fitz disconnected and looked at his two wide-eyed friends.

"That beats anythang I ever heard," Zee said.

"How can they have a warrant for your arrest?" Ben asked.

"I have no idea," Fitz said, searching his mind for an explanation. When he realized a probable possibility, he said, "Oh."

"Oh, what?" Ben replied.

"Crystal must have talked to the officer."

"So?" Ben said.

"So she made up a story that implicated me. She probably had Victor tell the police the same thing… and they believed them."

Fitz sat on the bed, his head hung low. "They believed them over me. It's just like when I was fired. They consider me expendable."

His heart sank into a dark place, like being swallowed in quicksand. Elbows on his knees, he rested his head in his hands and stared at the carpet.

"Hey. It's going to be OK. You have all of us to vouch for you," Ben said.

"Yeah. We don't consider you expendable," Zee added, patting him on the back.

The design in the carpet made it hard to focus. It seemed to fold into itself and worm around. Fitz's mind was worming around just like the carpet.

"I think I'm going to sit in the car with Buffett a while before I turn myself in," he muttered.

"You can't turn yourself in," Ben scolded. "You have to help us figure out how to nail these folks. There are a lot of lives depending on you. Just think of all the women she has in bondage."

Fitz did just that. He began to picture the faces of the women whom he had seen at Sparkles and thought about how they were stuck being forced to do something terrible. He looked up at Ben.

"That's better," Ben said. "Now, how could they convince the police that they are right and you were lying? Didn't they talk to Katía, too?"

"Crystal's an upstanding citizen. Influential in the community. I'm just a bum," Fitz mumbled.

"What about Katía? She's a pastor. That ought to pass as respectable," Zee protested.

"Crystal probably has connections on the force," Zee said.

"Wait, I'm the one who shot Victor. Why are they after you?" Ben wondered.

"That is interesting," Zee said.

"It's probably because I witnessed Victor's handiwork firsthand," Fitz said. "They needed to paint me as a villain since I survived his torture and her attempt to poison me."

"At least we know where she's keeping the drugs," Zee said.

Fitz and Ben looked at Zee, mouths open. "Where is she keeping the drugs?" Fitz asked.

"At the storage facility," Zee answered. "If she considers it safe enough to store hostages in, she'd think it's safe enough for the drugs."

"Zee, did anyone ever tell you you're a genius?" Ben said.

"Nah, I ain't never been called that before."

"It does make perfect sense," Fitz said. He combed through his beard with his fingers. Fatigue battled with the urge to get Crystal arrested and clear his name. A shocking thought hit.

"I have to get out of here," Fitz said.

"What are you talking about?"

"Geraldine has Zee's number. She would have to forward it on to the investigators so they could track me down."

"She wouldn't do that," Ben said.

"If she didn't, she'd risk being fired," Fitz replied.

"Surely they haven't had time to locate his phone yet," Ben said.

"I'm not sure I want to take that chance. I'd rather stay out of a jail cell." Fitz picked up the few things he had brought in with him.

"Where ya goin'?" Zee asked.

"First to get something to eat. I'm hungry. I haven't figured out where to go after that."

"You know, I'm hungry, too. I'll go with you," Ben said.

"Oh, man. I knew this was too good to be true," Zee groaned.

"You can stay here," Ben said. "I'll be back after a while.

Zee eyed the bed with longing. "Nah, I can't let my friends down."

CHAPTER 49

Turning out of the hotel parking lot, Fitz headed toward the closest Waffle House, which was off Mundy Mill Road near I-985. A tenth of a mile down the road, he noticed blue lights flashing. In the rearview mirror, he saw them turn into the hotel lot.

"That was close, Buffett. Would you stick with me even if I were a jailbird?"

Buffett purred. He was already settled in Fitz's lap. Fitz drove on, parked at the restaurant, and Ben and Zee pulled in right behind him.

"We probably should have told the others what's going on," Ben said, getting out of his car.

"They might have already been asleep. It would be a shame to wake them. Besides, they can honestly say they have no idea where we are if they're questioned," Fitz replied.

Fitz ordered pancakes and bacon. Zee and Ben both had eggs, bacon, and hashbrowns. Before Fitz started eating, he folded up one piece of bacon in a napkin.

"I bet that's for Buffett," Ben said.

"Yeah. He loves bacon," Fitz replied. He poured a lavish amount of syrup over his pancakes and dug in, his mind churning over how to stay out of jail.

"If they lock me up, will one of you take care of Buffett?"

After a brief hesitation, Ben said, "Of course we will. I'll be happy to take him in, but you're not going to prison."

"I hope not, but Crystal does seem to have connections in high places."

"We need a plan to reverse the tables and get her on the police's radar," Ben said.

"What if we just go find the drugs and call the police to the storage place?" Zee asked after a swallow of orange juice.

"There are a lot of units there," Ben observed.

"Not more than twenty to thirty. We might even get lucky and find them on the first try," Zee said.

"You're quite the optimist," Ben replied.

"She has connections in high places," Fitz said with a grin.

"You thought that was a problem a minute ago," Ben noted.

"I know what we have to do. Her ex is a lawyer with the district attorney's office. I just hope it was a nasty divorce battle," Fitz continued. "How long has it been since I shot out her tire?"

"Let's see." Ben rubbed his hand through his thinning hair. "We drove to the hotel, checked in, got to the room, and left. I'd say about an hour."

"That ought to be about enough time to get a road service out to change the tire. We need to time this just right." Fitz stuffed another bite of pancake into his mouth.

"Time what just right?" Ben asked.

"Yeah. You want to share what you're thinking?" Zee added.

"If I'm right, Crystal and I will get arrested together. Let's finish eating and go find those drugs.

As Fitz was paying at the counter, two police officers entered the restaurant. Fitz whispered, "Keep the change." He held his breath as he turned to walk out.

One of the officers glanced at him, and he nodded back. Fitz hurried out the door and stood by his car, watching to see if the officers would follow him.

Ben and Zee came out. "That was close," Zee chuckled.

They drove to the self-storage facility, the gate of which was still unlocked.

Fitz got out and began to refill Buffett's food and water.

"What are you doing?" Ben asked.

"I have to get Buffett set up. I might not see him for a long time. I have to scoop his litter."

"All right. I'll start cutting off the locks." Turning to Zee Ben said, "I guess we start at the beginning."

"If I was hidin' somethin' I wouldn't put it in the first place someone might look," Zee said.

"You're right. Let's start in the back. I'll cut the locks and you check the units."

Fitz finished scooping Buffett's litter and looked around for a trashcan. He heard the first rattle of a door being raised. Not seeing a can, he just set the bag by the fence.

Sitting back down in the car, he tapped his leg and Buffett hopped into his lap.

"They're going to haul me off tonight," he said, giving the cat an ear scratch. "Ben promised to take care of you till I get out. You might enjoy living in a house for a while."

Buffett seemed to sense Fitz's sadness and rubbed his chin.

"You've always been so good to me. You don't deserve to have to live in a car like this."

Buffett rubbed his chin along Fitz's chest, purring loudly, and snuggled down in his lap.

"I have no idea why you adopted me, but I'm thankful that you did. I wouldn't still be here without you."

Fitz petted him a moment longer, then said, "OK, I have an evil woman to trap."

Buffett hopped out of his lap, and Fitz joined Ben and Zee. They were on the eighth unit.

"No luck yet?" Fitz asked.

"Not yet, but we're just getting started," Ben said, grunting as he cut another padlock.

Zee walked out of the empty unit Ben had cut the lock off of previously. "Nothin' there either. Maybe I was wrong."

"We can't give up yet," Ben said as he moved to the next lock. He shook his hand after finishing the cut. "The next one's yours. My hands hurt."

Fitz took the cutter from Ben as Zee raised the door.

"I think we struck gold," Zee said.

He turned his phone's flashlight on and shined it at four plastic bins in the middle of the floor, stacked two by two. They hurried in, and Fitz pulled the top off one of the bins. Ben pulled off the other top.

"She has them separated by type," Ben noted.

"She's an organized soul," Zee said. "I wonder what all that is worth on the street."

"Don't get any ideas," Ben chuckled.

"I was just imaginin'," Zee replied.

"I think it's time to make a few phone calls," Fitz said.

CHAPTER 50

Fitz held his hand out to Zee. "Could I use your phone again?"

"Of course." He handed it over.

Fitz dialed the sheriff's office and asked for Geraldine.

"Hey, Geraldine. It's Fitz. I'm calling to let you know where I am so you can send someone to pick me up."

"You know I had to turn in that phone number," she replied.

"Yeah. No hard feelings. I'm at a self-storage facility on Atlanta Highway."

Ben called out the street number, and Fitz relayed it to Geraldine.

"Tell them to be careful. There's going to be a woman here trying to kill me. She'll be armed and dangerous," Fitz added.

"What have you gotten yourself into? Never mind. I don't want to know. Be careful… and don't leave this time."

Fitz disconnected and pulled up the Sparkles web site to find Crystal's number.

"I just had a great idea," Ben said. "Let's send her a text with our picture beside her drugs."

Zee laughed. "I love it!"

"Here's the number," Fitz said, handing the phone back to Zee so he could pull up the camera and text apps.

They posed beside the crates. Zee extended his long arm and said, "Say cheese," before snapping the photo. "You sure you want me to send this? It'd be safer to just let the police find her after they realize the drugs are here."

"I want to get this over with. Besides, don't you want to see the look on her face when they handcuff her?" Fitz replied.

"OK, if you say so." Zee typed, "Wishing you were here," into the text and hit send.

"Now let's find the ex-husband's number," Fitz said.

"I don't see any point in leaving this off any longer," Ben said as he powered up his phone.

Zee scrunched up his eyes. "You're not calling him this time of night, I hope."

"He's a DA. He's used to getting waked up in the middle of the night," Fitz replied.

"Got it," Ben said. "They have after-hours numbers listed. I assume you want to do the honors." He handed Fitz his phone.

Fitz memorized the number for Darryl Samson, then made the call.

"May I speak to Darryl Samson," he said to the sleepy-sounding man who answered.

"Speaking."

"I'm calling to let you know about some illegal activity in which Crystal Samson has been engaged."

"OK, you have my interest. What are you talking about?"

"We have discovered that she has been forcing undocumented women to steal opioids from clients so she can sell them. I believe her henchman has killed at least one person."

"That's quite a tale. I can't say that I'm surprised the witch would get into something nasty like that, but you need to be talking to the police."

"We have the police on their way. My question for you is would you grant immunity from deportation and prosecution in exchange for some of the workers testifying? She controlled the workers by threatening to deport them if they didn't steal the pills."

"I'm sure I could arrange that."

"Thank you so much. I apologize for waking you, but I needed to know before this all starts happening."

Fitz disconnected the call. "Well, I guess now we wait."

Fitz fished his car key out of his pocket and started to hand it to Ben. "Wait. I need to put my gun up."

"No, I think you'd better hang on to it. If Crystal gets here first, we might be in a fight for our lives," Ben said.

"True." Fitz handed over the key. "Make sure you get Buffett if they impound my car."

"I'll treat Buffett like a king, and I'll be there to pick you up when they realize their mistake," Ben replied. "In the meantime, we need to plan our cover in case Crystal attacks. All we have are our vehicles and the building. I think our safest bet is the vehicles."

Zee said, "We could get inside the unit and close the door. She'd have to be mighty brave to open it."

"Yeah, but I don't like not being able to see my pursuer," Ben replied. "I want to keep my eye on her."

Sirens sounded in the distance.

"I think the police will be here first," Zee said.

Blue lights began to strobe the trees at the front of the facility, then three patrol cars careened into the drive leading to the storage buildings.

"They're certainly not employing stealth in their approach," Ben observed.

The police totally blocked the entrance with their vehicles, then hurried toward the buildings. One officer called, "Joe Fitzgerald, you're under arrest. Come out with your hands up."

Fitz called, "We're in the back. There's something you need to see back here." He handed Zee his Beretta.

The three officers reached the corner of the building in front of where Fitz, Ben, and Zee were standing. "Hands up," he called.

The three complied, and the officers approached.

"That is you, isn't it, Fitz?" one officer, pudgy with blond hair, said. "I'm not surprised. You have a reputation as a troublemaker. You're under arrest for the attempted murder of Victor Pelfrey. Put your hands behind you."

While cuffing him, the officer said, "You have the right to remain silent. Anything you say can and will be used against you in a court of law. You have the right to an attorney. If you can't afford one, one will be appointed for you. Do you understand your rights?"

"I understand, Dan. Now, what you need to see is in the open unit behind me. Crystal Samson has been forcing the workers in her cleaning business to steal opioids, and she sells them. We found her stash," Fitz responded.

"I find that hard to believe, Fitz. She's a fine, upstanding member of the community," Dan said, grabbing one of Fitz's arms and dragging him forward.

"Of course you won't believe me if you don't look," Fitz replied.

Dan stopped. "OK, we'll play your little game. Chase, see what's in the unit."

Chase ducked inside while Mike, the third officer, kept an eye on Ben and Zee.

"Holy mackerel! You have to see this."

They heard Chase shifting the bins around.

"There are four bins full of opioids," Chase called. "We could sell this and retire!"

Dan glared at Fitz, then apparently decided he wanted to see for himself. "OK, let's move into the unit." He gave Fitz a little shove.

Mike ordered Ben and Zee into the unit, and they all converged around the four open bins.

"Wow. That's a lot of pills," Mike said.

"Shall we add this to your list of charges, Fitz?" Dan sneered.

Fitz responded, "I don't think so. If you're responsible enough to look into it, you'll find that this place belongs to Crystal Samson. She's the one you need to be arresting."

"She and her sidekick, Shannon," Zee added. "We have a whole group of folks who know the truth and are willing to testify. We're also willing to testify as to how you handle discovering these drugs."

Zee's comment drew an angry glare from Dan. "Watch your mouth."

"I cain't see it without a mirror," Zee replied.

Dan's teeth gritted, and his fist clenched. After a moment of tense silence, he said, "Get the narc squad down here. You three sit down against the building and don't move. I've been chasing you around all night, and you're not getting away."

Fitz eased himself down, using the side of the building to help since his hands were cuffed behind him. Ben and Zee joined him. "Do you think we should warn them about Crystal being on her way?" Ben asked.

"Probably," Fitz answered.

Ben spoke up, "We're expecting Crystal and Shannon to be here any minute. They are armed, so be careful."

"And just how do you know that?" Dan asked.

"She has been chasing us and trying to kill us for two days. We sent her a picture of us standing by her cache of drugs. She'll be here."

While Ben was talking, Fitz noticed car lights slowing down on the road in front of the storage facility.

"In fact, I think that's her right now," Fitz said.

"Yeah, right," Dan said, looking toward the road.

The car accelerated and zoomed out of sight.

"There she goes," Fitz said. "She has been driving a BMW tonight. If you go after her, you should know she has an assault rifle and a hunting rifle."

Dan eyed Fitz, and Fitz could tell he was weighing whether or not to believe him.

"Do you want me to pursue?" Mike asked.

Dan hesitated. Finally he said, "No, let's let the narcs sort this out before we go arresting a prominent member of the community. Besides, that was probably just someone about to make a wrong turn."

Fitz rolled his eyes.

CHAPTER 51

About twenty minutes later, a detective rolled up to the storage facility where the officers were waiting with Fitz, Ben, and Zee. The detective stood up out of the car, stretched, then retrieved a coffee thermos. She was a short, fit forty-five year-old woman with wavy brown hair and brown eyes.

"Merilyn Masters. Nice to meet you. What have we got here?" she said as she walked up to the officers and shook their hands.

She glanced over at the three men sitting against the building. "Are these the perps?"

"They claim not," Dan said.

"Don't they always?" Merilyn chuckled.

"We found four bins full of what looks like opioids," Dan said, leading her into the unit.

She shined a flashlight into the bins. "Looks like oxy and hydro. What's the story?"

"They claim a prominent citizen is using undocumented immigrants to steal them from clients of her cleaning service and then selling them. They say they found out about this, and she has been trying to kill them ever since," Dan explained. "Fitz Fitzgerald, the one with the scraggly beard, is wanted for attempted murder."

Fitz watched as she held her chin in one hand, apparently thinking.

"I see. Do you guys mind hanging around long enough for me to question these three?"

"We don't have anything better to do," Dan answered.

"Thanks. Oh, let me get my camera so one of you can take pictures before we load up the drugs."

Merilyn returned with the camera and handed it off to Mike. She studied the three men, then asked Ben to come with her. She led him far enough away so the others couldn't hear them.

While she was talking to Ben, Fitz whispered to Zee, "Just tell her the truth."

"That's my plan," Zee replied.

After questioning Ben and Zee, she called Fitz to come with her. Chase came along since he was a wanted felon.

"According to your friends, you didn't shoot anybody," Merilyn began. "That remains to be seen, because we know friends are loyal. The one guy even claims he shot the victim in self-defense."

Fitz listened, wondering where she was going with her statements.

"We will be doing ballistics tests, of course. The results will at least let us know which gun the bullets were fired from. I'm assuming your story is going to be the same as the others but go ahead and tell me what happened."

Starting with meeting Victoria in the park, Fitz related the whole series of events that had led them to this point. All the time he was trying to gauge whether she believed him. He finished with, "As you see, we tried to lure Crystal Samson here. She started to turn in but took off when she saw the police cars. She's on the run now."

"Thank you very much, Mr. Fitzgerald.

Merilyn led him back to the others and talked with the officers. "I'm inclined to believe them. There is enough variation in the stories that they didn't seem rehearsed, but the details all match up."

"That's all well and good, but we still have to arrest this guy. We have a warrant," Dan said.

"I know. I'm going to try to get arrest warrants for Crystal Samson, Shannon Bledsoe, and Victor Pelfrey. Oh, they claim Pelfrey said he's part of the Cañería cartel. Get the word out to be watching for them to show up."

"I hope not. They're big trouble," Chase said.

Merilyn replied, "Yeah. In the meantime, let's get these drugs to the precinct. I want two of you to deliver them so there are no questions. Watch them being placed into the car, and whoever's transporting them, wait until the other one is there before you pull them out. Got it?"

"Got it," Dan said.

"Mr. Fitzgerald, you have a date with these guys at the precinct. Mr. Blessing, could I have the gun you claim you used to shoot Mr. Pelfrey?" Merilyn asked, realizing with a cringe that she hadn't checked to see if they had any weapons.

Ben handed over his handgun.

"You and Mr. Jameson are free to go. I have your contact information if we have any further questions."

Chase led Fitz to his patrol car. "I've got the perp if you two will handle the drugs."

"I'm not 'the perp,'" Fitz said. "I have a name and technically I'm a suspect."

"Whatever," Chase said, opening the back door.

Fitz looked back to Ben and Zee. "Don't forget Buffett."

"We've got him. We'll take care of your car, too," Ben called back.

"And see if you can find Crystal. She's probably going to run.," Fitz called as the door was shutting.

He sighed as Chase got into the driver's seat. The stress of having his hands cuffed behind him put a strain on the wounds. His heart hurt worse, though. He had never been on this end of an arrest, though he'd often wondered what it was like. He wasn't enjoying finding out.

He saw Buffett looking out the window as the patrol car drove away into the night. *I'm going to miss my little buddy. I wonder what time it is.*

Ben checked his watch as the patrol car drove away with Fitz. It was 3:37am. He was trying to figure their next step when Dan called from his patrol car, "You folks do have to leave, you know."

"Got it," Ben answered, then turned to Zee, "Let's go back to the hotel, park a car, then come back for Buffett. Then we'll figure out what to do next."

"Sounds good to me," Zee replied.

They parked Zee's car at the hotel, then returned and picked up Fitz's. Ben checked Buffett's water and added more food. The litter was still clean from when Fitz had scooped it earlier. They headed up to the room.

"I'm not sure how much longer this old body can keep going," Zee said.

"I know what you mean. I wonder what they're going to do with Fitz.

"I know exactly what they'll do. They'll take him to the station, book him, and put him in a cell. The detective will probably come by and ask more questions."

"That sounds like the voice of experience."

Zee just grinned.

"I think there's a coffee machine in the lobby. We need to tank up and get going," Ben said.

"Where we goin'?" Zee asked.

"I'm betting Crystal either went to Sparkles or home. If I were her, I'd get packing so I could get out of town and disappear."

"Yeah, that's what I'd do. Of course, I wouldn't have to go pack," Zee chuckled.

They located the Keurig coffee maker, brewed two cups, and took off.

"I'm just going to leave King here," Zee said.

They hopped into Ben's car. Snickers was asleep in the back seat.

"Let's pass by Sparkles just in case, then head to her house. You work on finding her address and getting it mapped on the way."

Ben drove to Sparkles, which was ten minutes from the hotel. The parking lot was empty and the building dark.

"She must be at the house. I hope we're not too late," Ben said.

CHAPTER 52

Ben approached Crystal's house, and the app on Zee's phone said, "Your destination is on the right."

"That's it," Zee said. "I see the BMW in the garage."

"I wasn't expecting her to have company, though," Ben said.

A low-rider Cadillac with lots of bling was parked in the driveway. Ben parked on the side of the road just past the house. It was an impressive two-story brick house with a three-car garage. The bay containing the BMW was open.

Ben rolled down his window. Shouting came from the house, but he couldn't make out what was being said.

"Somebody's not happy," he said. "Think it's a lover's spat?"

"Nah, I think it's a shake-down. She's gone and gotten herself in trouble with a dealer, I bet."

Ben resented the wave of concern that hit. "I guess she deserves what she gets," he said, wishing he meant it.

The crack of a gunshot split the night air. The next words that came from the house were loud and unmistakable: "I want my pills now, or the next one goes through your head!"

"We have to do something," Ben whispered.

"I thought you just said she deserves what she gets. If we let this play out, we might not need the police," Zee replied.

"Come on. We can't let him kill her, even if she is a witch. You still have the Beretta?"

"Yeah."

Ben opened the door and slid out of the car. He led Zee along woods at the side of the house.

"I mean it, woman! I need those pills tonight!" came through the window as Ben crossed the front yard, heading toward the garage.

"I told you the police found the stash! There's nothing I can do about it right now!" Crystal screamed.

Ben and Zee crouched beside the garage.

"We could shoot out his tires. That should get his attention," Ben whispered.

"No, man. We want this guy to be able to leave," Zee replied.

"I think we need to go in before he kills her."

"I can't believe you want to rescue her after all she's done."

"Me, either, but it's the right thing to do."

Ben started inside the garage, his heart thudding, when he heard Crystal scream, "Get your hands off me!"

"You're coming with me to a nice, lonely place," the guy said.

"Let go of my arm!"

"You can come quietly, or we'll get blood all over your nice house."

There was silence, and Ben took a few more steps toward the door. The sound of footsteps stopped him.

"Get back," he whispered to Zee, and they retreated out of the garage.

Just as they crouched in the darkness, the door opened. Ben could hear his heart pounding. He watched as the guy followed Crystal to his car, a handgun jabbed in her back. He turned to Zee and held a finger to his lips. He held out his hand, and Zee gave him the Beretta.

Ben crept up behind the guy. He grabbed the guy's collar, shoved the pistol to his head, and growled, "Drop the gun."

The guy jumped so with shock that his gun flew out of his hand. Zee moseyed over and picked it up.

"Thanks for being so cooperative," Zee said.

"What the… It's you! What are you doing here?" Crystal stammered.

"Saving your life for one thing," Ben said. "A simple thank you will do."

Zee had his phone to his ear. "I'm reporting an armed burglary. … Right now, we have the suspect under control. …" He put his hand over the mic, "Hey, what's the address here?"

The guy tried to pull away from Ben, and Ben pushed the gun into his head harder. "Don't make me slip and pull the trigger. Get on the ground."

While Zee continued with the 911 call, Ben put his knee on the guy's back, handed Zee the gun, fished out zip-ties from his coat pocket, and said, "Hands behind your back."

A sound drew Ben's attention while he was trying to get the zip-ties on the guy. A garage door was opening. The Corvette fired up and screeched out of the garage as soon as the door was high enough.

"Zee, shoot out her tires!" Ben yelled.

"Hold on a minute," Zee told the operator. He aimed and fired, getting off three rounds before she was out of sight. Each shot missed its mark.

"Yeah, that was gunfire. Crystal just got away. … She's a drug supplier you need to be arresting."

"Come on! We have to follow her." Ben bent down to the guy on the ground. "You stay put till the police get here."

Ben and Zee hurried to Ben's car as fast as two old men could and took off after Crystal.

"While you've got 911 on the line, tell them about our pursuit of Crystal," Ben said.

Ben saw the Corvette's taillights flash, then it turned left out of the subdivision. He accelerated, trying to catch up.

Zee disconnected the 911 call and said, "You know you cain't keep up with that Vette, right?"

"I can if she's going the speed limit so she doesn't get pulled over. What did they say about our following Crystal?"

Zee replied, "She said we'd better leave her alone."

"That's not going to happen."

Ben slowed, checked for oncoming vehicles, and turned left onto Ledan Road. He glimpsed the Corvette's taillights going over a hill and pressed the accelerator not quite to the floor. His heart was still pounding.

"For Fitz's sake, we can't let her get away," Ben growled as the engine roared.

"Where do you think she's going?" Zee asked.

"If I were me, I'd go to the airport and fly out of the country."

"That means she'll get on the expressway. She'll leave us in her dust."

"I don't think she'll risk a speeding ticket, do you? Besides, I hope to catch her before then."

Topping the hill, Ben saw the Corvette exit the traffic circle, going right onto Sardis Road.

"That's not the way to the expressway," Zee observed.

"Nope. I wonder what she's up to."

Ben steered his car into the traffic circle and out the first exit. He followed so he could just see the taillights ahead. She turned right onto Short Road, right onto Price Road, then right into a subdivision.

"I bet she's going to pick up Shannon," Ben surmised.

"I bet you're right. They're going to make a run for it like Butch Cassidy and the Sundance Kid."

"I hope it doesn't come to that," Ben replied. "I wonder if she suspects we're following her."

"She doesn't act like it," Zee answered.

When he saw the Corvette turn into a driveway, Ben pulled to the side of the road and cut his lights.

"Now what?" Zee asked.

CHAPTER 53

Ben and Zee watched as Crystal got out of the Corvette and walked to the door.

"Call 911 and tell them where we are," Ben said.

Zee placed the call. "I'd like to report the whereabouts of a criminal. ... We're on Walnut Grove Way. ... I don't know the exact address, but there's a white Corvette in the driveway. ... Yeah, I'm the same person who called a little bit ago. ... That'll work." He disconnected. "They're sending an officer to arrest us for stalking."

"At least that'll get them here."

"That's what I told her."

Crystal stepped inside and closed the door.

"I have a plan," Ben said. He pulled his Outback down and blocked the driveway. Cutting the engine, he said. "Let's get out of here and hide by the house. She's liable to start shooting."

They exited the car and hurried around to the side of the garage. Ben noticed his heart pounding again. "I'm getting too old for this much excitement," he whispered to Zee.

"Tell me about it. I'm gonna sleep for a week when this is over."

"You're not packed yet?" Crystal screamed. "I'm leaving without you if you don't come on right now. I'm not missing that plane."

"OK. OK. I'm coming," Shannon replied.

"A dealer showed up at my house demanding drugs before I left. Then two of those old goofballs showed up, too. We have to get out of here."

Ben whispered to Zee, "Get ready, I think they're coming."

They heard the front door open. "What is that?" Shannon asked.

"It's that old guy's car. They followed me!"

The report of three gunshots and glass exploding made Ben jump.

"Go see if I hit them," Crystal said.

"Are you crazy? I'm not walking up to that car. Let's just go. You can pull through the yard."

"If I didn't kill them, they could shoot us as we drive by," Crystal said.

"And you want me just to walk up to the car and hope they don't shoot? You're insane. Besides, if they were going to shoot us, they'd have already fired. You must have hit them."

"OK. Let's go."

Ben whispered, "We have to do something."

Zee shrugged his shoulders.

Ben peeked around the side of the house. As soon as Crystal was about to reach for the car door and Shannon was walking around the front of the car, he yelled, "Don't move and drop the guns!"

He saw Crystal jump, then she leveled her pistol and fired. Ben jumped back behind the house just in time.

"Get in!" Crystal ordered and fired two more times.

Ben heard the Corvette fire up. He made a move to step out but was stopped by another gunshot. He waited till he heard the car moving, stepped just around the corner and shot out the two back tires.

Crystal kept driving through the yard and off the curb. With the tires deflated, the car was so low it got hung on the curb.

"You don't see that every day," Zee observed.

When the doors of the Corvette opened, Ben and Zee ducked back behind the house. Two bullets hit the corner, splintering the wood.

"I hope you got the key out of your car," Zee said.

"Yeah, it's in my pocket." Ben peeked out to see Crystal and Shannon running up the driveway and pulling suitcases. She fired at him again, then they hurried into the house.

"I sure wish the police would show up about now," Zee said.

As soon as he finished, blue light began to strobe the side of the house. The patrol car drove down the street toward them, making them visible to the officers.

"I'm pretty sure they've seen us, so there's no point in hiding," Ben said.

The patrol car stopped behind Ben's Outback. Ben couldn't see the officers through the window. When they didn't get out, he got worried.

The sound of sirens preceded the arrival of two more patrol cars.

"We're gettin' a lot of attention," Zee said.

Two officers jumped out of the first car that arrived. The one on the passenger side rounded the vehicle, and they both crouched behind it.

The sudden blast of a spotlight nearly blinded Ben.

"Come out with your hands up," The officer yelled.

Ben raised his hands and called back, "Officer, there are two women in the house who are armed and are trying to kill us. I'm afraid they'll shoot if we walk to you."

"That's not the story I heard. You have been stalking and harassing them," the officer called back.

Ben replied, "While that is technically true, these women are drug suppliers. Their stash was confiscated a couple of hours ago. There should be a warrant for their arrest by now. They're Crystal Samson and Shannon Bledsoe."

"That's a likely story," the officer said. "Now come on out and lie face down on the driveway."

Ben hesitated.

"Now!" The officer yelled.

Ben whispered to Zee, "Stay close to the garage door so they won't have a direct shot." Ben laid his gun on the driveway, then lay down right next to the garage door. Zee followed, doing the same thing.

"Hey, Ray, they're right. There is a warrant for the arrest of the two women he mentioned, and this is where one of them lives. They're considered armed and dangerous," Ben heard one of the other officers say.

"Everyone, take cover. Jeff and Diann, take the back of the house. Someone get me a bullhorn," the officer named Ray ordered.

Ben heard the footsteps of two officers running past him.

"You think they'll give up?" Zee asked.

Just as he said that, the garage door began opening. Ben could hear the car running.

"They'll run over us. We have to move," he yelled. Without waiting for an answer from the police, he jumped up, pulled Zee up, and ran to the side of the house.

The engine roared, and Shannon's Camry came flying out, scraping the roof on the bottom of the garage door. As she turned to drive through the yard, an officer pulled a patrol car up and blocked the remaining space between the Corvette and a line of trees. Shannon skidded and plowed into the side of the patrol car.

The two officers who had gone to the back of the house came running. "Get down, you idiots," Diann yelled to Ben and Zee. The two officers stopped at the corner of the house, and Ben and Zee stepped behind them.

Ben heard, "Get out of the car with your hands up!" He realized he had his fists clenched and tried to relax.

After a tense silence, Ben heard the car doors open.

"Step out and put your hands on the trunk! And keep them there!" An officer commanded.

"You are under arrest for drug trafficking, firing a gun in a residential area, and I'm sure there will be more charges forthcoming. You have the right to remain silent…"

Ben sighed and stepped onto the driveway. "She shot up my car," he groaned.

"You two aren't going anywhere. I'm taking you in, too," the officer named Diann said.

"What for?" Ben asked.

"I'm not sure, but there has to be something. You've caused enough trouble for one night."

CHAPTER 54

It was 5:54 as Ray and Jeff led Crystal and Shannon into the police precinct ahead of Ben and Zee. A rosy glow was just beginning to break the darkness. Crystal was still screaming. "You can't arrest me! Don't you know who I am? I demand to see my lawyer! Get your hands off me!"

Diann led Ben and Zee to a holding cell while Ray and Jeff led the two women to another cell.

"We thought we'd join you," Ben said when he saw Fitz sitting in the cell. There were two other men in the cell with him.

"You shouldn't have," Fitz said. "I see they finally caught Crystal and Shannon." A wave of satisfaction moved his angst aside for a moment.

"Yeah. How ya doin'?" Zee asked.

"Mostly I've been sitting here worrying…. Worrying about y'all. Worrying that Crystal would get away with this. Worrying about Katía. I hope she's going to be all right. Wait, what happened to Buffett?"

"First of all, Buffett is in your car at the hotel. Secondly, Katía will be fine," Ben replied. "She's in good shape, and the wound only required some stitches."

"I was more worried about her emotional state. Getting shot can take a lot out of you. How are y'all doing?"

"Other than being dog tired, I'm good. How about you, Ben?" Zee replied.

"I'm good. You missed quite a show. If we weren't so agile, Shannon would have run over us."

Zee laughed. "I ain't never been described as agile before."

Zee and Ben proceeded to tell the story of how they had followed Crystal and ended up in the holding cell.

"Your night has been more exciting than mine," Fitz said.

"They say no good deed goes unpunished. How long do you think we're going to be behind bars?" Ben asked.

"I have no idea," Fitz replied.

"I have a good feeling about this. I think we'll be out today," Zee said. "You been booked yet?"

"Not yet. I've just been sitting here waiting," Fitz said. Seeing the sky lighten brought an urge to get back to his daily routine. It was time to go to the park, wash up, and tend to Buffett. "I need to get out of here."

"We will. We just have to let the wheels of justice turn," Zee said.

At 7:24am a man dressed in a charcoal gray suit walked in.

"It looks like somebody's lawyer's here," Zee observed.

With nothing else to do, Fitz watched as the man talked with the officer at the desk. After a brief conversation, the man walked toward the holding cell. Holding up a piece of paper, he said, "I need Joe Fitzgerald, Ben Blessing, and Zee Jameson, please.

The three of them stood up and walked forward.

"I'm Darryl Samson. I spoke with Joe on the phone in the middle of the night."

"I'm Joe, but most people call me Fitz."

"First of all, I want to thank the three of you for exposing my ex's illegal drug activity and helping to catch her. She's a piece of work, and I'm thankful I got out of the marriage before she got into the drug business. I always wondered how she lived so lavishly on the income she made from Sparkles.

"Anyway, I'm happy to say that the DA has agreed to grant immunity to any of her workers who will testify. I'm also happy to say that the three of you will be released as soon as they can find the key."

"They lost the key?" Zee gasped.

"Not exactly. The officer who has it apparently went to the restroom. He'll be back soon. I do need to ask if you can direct me to any of the workers who would be willing to testify."

Fitz smiled. "We just happen to know where two of them are hiding right now."

"Looking for this?" an officer said, walking up with the key to the cell.

Darryl waited as the officer let them out and they obtained their personal items.

"Where are we going?" he asked as they walked toward the door.

"I don't guess we're going anywhere," Zee said. "They didn't let us bring our cars."

"If you'll direct, I'll drive. How's that?" Darryl answered.

"Perfect. We're going to the Jameson Inn in Oakwood," Fitz said.

"I'd like to stop by Shannon's and pick up what's left of my car," Ben said. "I can take us from there, if it runs.

The Outback's only problem seemed to be that the windows were shot out, so Ben drove it to the hotel.

"I guess I'll be calling the repair folks again," Ben groaned before getting in.

"It's a good thing we left Snickers with King," Zee added.

Walking up to the room Katía and María were in, Fitz heard Katía say, "What do you mean they're not in the room? Where did they go?"

"I have no idea," Luna responded.

Fitz knocked on the door. Katía opened it, and her eyes went wide.

"Where were you? Don't scare us like that!" Then she surged forward and grabbed him in a hug.

Fitz groaned with pain, then hugged her back. "We have a long story to tell."

*　*　*　*　*

Three days later, Luna and Katía were already busy in Luna's kitchen preparing bread and salad to go with the lasagna when the others began to arrive. Fitz, Ben, and Zee arrived together. Ben had insisted that Fitz and Zee stay at his house at least till Fitz's wounds healed.

Katía answered the door. "Howdy, partners!" She held the door as the three men entered, then wrapped her arm around Fitz and gave him a sideways hug. "Are those wounds any better?"

He patted her hand and answered, "Getting better every day. How about your arm?"

"It's still sore, but it's not slowing me down, unless I try to reach something up high."

"I'm sorry you got hurt," Fitz said for at least the fortieth time.

"You can quit saying that, you know. We're going to be OK."

"Wow! Somethin' smells scrumptious!" Zee said.

A knock on the door revealed Victoria, Alejandro, and Sophía. They had brought María along, too.

Luna pulled the bread out of the oven and announced, "Everything is ready. Let's eat!"

They gathered around her dining room table. Carlos raised his glass and said, "Here's to the park pals and all the lives they saved through their bravery and cunning!"

"Amen!" Victoria said.

Katía said the blessing, and they all sat down to eat. Fitz looked around at the faces in the room, and his heart warmed.

I like my new family.

A NOTE FROM THE AUTHOR

I really appreciate you for investing your time in reading this book and trust it was enjoyable. It would mean a lot to me if you would take a moment to go to the site from which you purchased the novel and leave a review or at least a rating.

If you missed the first book in the Park Pals Myster series, *The Hidden Scalpel,* it can be found wherever you purchased this book.

The third book in this series is in the works and should be released by the end of 2025 or early 2026. If you'd like to be notified when it is released please go to www.DwainWrites.com and indicate that on the communication form. Happy reading!

ACKNOWLEDGEMENTS

While writing a novel involves a lot of time sitting alone at the computer, it also requires a village. I am so grateful to the people who have helped me with *The Missing Pill!*

Alan Edwards, the pharmacist for Good News Clinic was instrumental in helping me to understand what a person would go through if they couldn't afford medication and utilized the clinic, which provides medical services to Hall County's struggling population. Shean Brown, a pharmacist at Walgreens gave his time to help figure out the cost of Victoria's medication if she were to purchase it without a prescription. He surprised me by coming up with a way that it wasn't terribly expensive.

B. J. Myers-Bradley, Clara Bella Rose, and Yvette Summerour were amazingly helpful by reading through the manuscript and providing feedback. I deeply appreciate their time and insights. Each of them helped to make *The Missing Pill* a better book.

A huge thank you goes out the Merilyn Guerry, who applied her highly honed editorial skills to sharpening the manuscript to improve the book's quality. I am grateful to her for the time and energy she poured into this project.

I am grateful for the artistic skills of Becky Franks for the author photo and Getcovers for the cover design.

OTHER BOOKS BY DWAIN CASSADY

THE PARK PALS SERIES:
THE HIDDEN SCALPEL

THE DARK WINGS TRILOGY:
DARK WINGS RISING
DARK WINGS DARING
DARK WINGS SOARING

THE WILLOW NOVELS:
FEATHERS IN WATER
FEATHERS IN FLIGHT

ADVENT DEVOTIONALS:
INSIGHTS FROM MATTHEW
PRESENCE IN THE MANGER
THE COMING LIGHT
THE SOIL OF SALVATION